Chapter One

"Why exactly did we come this way, Tris?" Andi Talbot demanded as a heavy lorry rumbled past on the main road. "Buddy's getting freaked out by all this traffic." The little Jack Russell terrier trotting beside her leapt to the end of his lead, barking madly. She reached down to smooth the fur between his ears.

"Because the best car park in the whole of Lancaster for skateboarding is up here," Tristan replied. "It's wide and smooth, with no manhole covers. Perfect for practising jumps."

"It's a shame it won't have the best skate*boarder* in Lancaster on it," added Natalie Lewis, their best friend.

Making a face at her, Tristan pushed off and sent his skateboard rolling along the tarmac in front of them. He picked up speed, then leapt off his board

1

and twisted his whole body round. Landing perfectly on the board again, he punched his fists up into the air triumphantly. "At this rate, I'll be able to turn professional!"

"Wow!" Andi said, impressed.

"My best yet," he agreed, picking up his board and walking back. He bent down to stroke Buddy. The terrier had stopped barking but he still watched the racing traffic closely, flinching when big lorries passed.

"I bet it was a fluke," said Natalie. "Bet you can't do it again." She flipped her blonde hair out of her eyes and laughed. "I can see a spectacular skateboard crash coming up any minute now."

Tristan frowned. "I'll do even better this time."

"You'll fall off," Natalie warned.

Tristan stepped on to the board and began to race away.

Andi and Natalie exchanged doubtful glances. "He'll end up breaking his arm or something," Natalie said, as he sprang into the air again. She bent down and covered her black Labrador's eyes with her hand. "Don't look, Jet," she joked.

Tristan spun around again, but this time, he missed the skateboard completely on the way down. His

THE PET FINDERS CLUB

The Dog With
No Name

BEN M. BAGLIO

*Hodder
Children's
Books*

A division of Hachette Children's Books

Special thanks to Liss Norton

Text copyright © 2005 Working Partners Ltd
Illustration copyright © 2008 Cecilia Johansson

First published in the USA in 2005 by Scholastic Inc

First published in Great Britain in 2008
by Hodder Children's Books

The rights of Ben M Baglio and Cecilia Johansson to be identified
as the Author and Illustrator of the Work respectively have
been asserted by them in accordance with the Copyright,
Designs and Patents Act 1988

1

ISBN 978 0 340 93134 9

Typeset in Weiss by Avon DataSet Ltd,
Bidford on Avon, Warwickshire

Printed in the UK by CPI Bookmarque, Croydon, CR0 4TD

The paper and board used in this paperback by Hodder Children's
Books are natural recyclable products made from wood grown in
sustainable forests. The manufacturing processes conform to the
environmental regulations of the country of origin.

Hodder Children's Books
a division of Hachette Children's Books
338 Euston Road, London NW1 3BH
An Hachette Livre UK company

ankle crumpled underneath him and he staggered backwards, flapping his arms as he tried to keep his balance. He stumbled on the steeply-sloping verge that bordered the pavement, and went rolling down the grass and out of sight.

Andi and Natalie rushed over with the dogs scampering beside them.

"Are you all right?" Andi called.

There was no reply.

"Tristan!" She reached the place where Tristan had disappeared, then stopped and stared. He was crawling out of a water-filled ditch at the bottom of the slope, his hair and clothes covered with sticky grey mud.

Natalie stood beside Andi, open-mouthed.

"I'm all right!" he called up to them, wiping away streaks of grime from his face. "Not hurt at all – in case you were worried."

"Doing your swamp creature impersonation?" Natalie said.

"Something like that."

"Come on, let's give him a hand," Andi said, trying not to laugh. Wet muck was dripping from his hair and there was a piece of feathery pondweed stuck to his shoulder.

She began to scramble down the bank towards Tristan.

"I'll only help if he promises not to touch my jacket," Natalie said, stepping carefully after her. Jet and Buddy bounced along on their leads beside the girls, as if the ditch was a much more interesting place to be than the pavement.

By the time Andi reached Tristan, he was kneeling beside the ditch, wiping his hands on the grass. "Yuck! Look at this stuff!"

"It's called mud, Tristan," Natalie puffed, sliding down the last few feet to join them. "And it's not toxic."

"Do you need a hand standing up?" Andi offered.

"Not until I've emptied my trainers. There's something wriggling around in one of them. I think I've caught a tadpole."

"Gross!" Natalie moaned. Then her face turned very serious. "Be really careful when you take your shoes off, Tris."

Andi and Tristan stared at her.

"Why?" Tristan asked nervously, stopping in the middle of untying his lace.

"It might not be a tadpole. It might be a fish." Natalie grinned. "I just thought you might want to save it for your mid-morning snack. I mean, it must be an hour and a half since you had anything to eat."

"Very funny!" Tristan made a face at Natalie. "I don't eat *that* much."

"That's not really true, is it, Tris?" Andi pointed out. Tristan was famous for being hungry. He knew just about every café and corner shop in Aldcliffe, the suburb of Lancaster where they all lived. She was about to remind him of a time when he'd eaten a family-sized bag of crisps all in one go, when Buddy began to whine and pull on his lead.

"What's up, Bud?" Andi asked, looking down at the tan-and-white terrier. "Can't you stand seeing Tristan like this?"

Buddy's whine became more urgent. He looked up at Andi and barked sharply.

"What is it, boy?"

"He's probably picked up the scent of a pizza box again," Natalie said. "Let's get back to the pavement before we end up looking like Tris."

"No, wait. This feels like something different." Andi let Buddy drag her along the bank towards a clump of rough, thorny shrubs.

"What's he found?" Tristan wondered as Buddy rushed up to the bushes, sniffing eagerly.

"I don't know. It could be a duck or something."

Andi pulled the sleeves of her jacket down to protect her hands, then pushed her way into the shrubs. Through the dense branches and brambles, she could see something lying at the edge of the ditch, but it was entirely covered in mud so that she couldn't make out what it was. An old sweater? Someone's old shopping bag?

Buddy looked up at her and whined. Would he really be this interested in a piece of rubbish? Andi bent down and pushed some long grass aside to see more clearly, then jumped back, shocked. It was a puppy, lying horrifyingly still. "Oh no!" she gasped.

"What is it?" Natalie called, making her way over. Tristan came limping after her, holding one trainer in his hand.

"There's a puppy in there," Andi gulped. She parted the branches again and they all peered through. The puppy was lying half in and half out of the ditch. You couldn't even tell what colour it was, underneath all the mud.

"Do you think it's – dead?" Natalie whispered.

Before anyone could reply, Buddy quickly made his way through the bushes and touched the puppy's face with his nose. The puppy whimpered weakly and opened one eye.

6

"It's alive!" Tristan exclaimed. "Come on, we've got to get it out." He threw down his trainer and shoved his way into the shrubs, holding his hands above his head to save himself from being pricked by the occasional thorn.

Natalie pulled out her mobile phone. "I'll ring Fisher." Fisher Pearce was the vet at the local RSPCA centre, and they knew him well. They often bumped into him around the town. He was a good friend of Christine Wilson, Tristan's mum's cousin, who also owned a local pet shop.

"Can you hold Buddy too, Nat?" Andi asked. "I want to help Tris." When Natalie nodded, her mobile phone clamped to one ear, Andi handed her Buddy's lead and quickly began trampling through the bushes.

The puppy's ears twitched as they knelt beside her. "I think she's a Labrador," Andi said. "She's got those thick, floppy ears that Labradors have and she looks pretty muscular under all that mud." Andi rested her hand on the puppy's broad, rounded forehead; she felt very cold. A tiny pink tongue flicked out under the puppy's nose, as if she wanted to lick Andi's hand.

"It's all right, little one," Andi whispered. "We're going to get you out of here."

Tristan wriggled further into the bushes, then slid

down into the ditch, wading through the thigh-deep muddy water until he was behind her. "I'll lift her from here. That way—" He broke off. "Hang on! Her back leg's twisted. I don't think we should move her."

"We can't leave her like this!" Andi protested. "She's so cold. Can't we at least lift her out of the thorns?"

"No. It could cause more damage. Let's wait for Fisher."

Andi took off her jacket and laid it over the puppy. "Don't worry, girl," she said. "You'll be safe soon." She cleared mud away from the tiny Labrador's nose so she could breathe more easily, then gently slid her hand under her ribcage, feeling for her heartbeat. She could just make out a faint flutter, but it was nothing like the strong, steady pulse she felt when Buddy lay across her lap.

"I hope Fisher gets here quickly," she said. She could hear Natalie talking into the phone, but she couldn't make out what she was saying above the roar of the traffic on the road above them.

"Do you think she was hit by a car?" Andi wondered, stroking the tiny creature's head.

"Probably," Tristan agreed. "Poor little scrap. From the look of all that mud, she must have fallen right into the ditch. She's lucky she managed to pull herself out, or she might have drowned, with all this rain we've had."

"I wonder why she was out alone on this busy road," Andi said.

Tristan shrugged. "Who knows?" He was shivering violently.

"Come out of the ditch, Tris," Andi said. "You look frozen. I know it's spring, but it's not that warm today."

Tristan clambered out, his single trainer squelching and murky water dripping from his jeans. "I feel so useless," he muttered, staring down at the motionless puppy.

"Me too." Andi felt a stab of fear. What if the puppy had died while they'd been talking? She reached under the dog's cold body again, but to her relief the little heart was still beating, though it felt even weaker and more irregular than before. "Hold on, girl!" she whispered.

"We'll have to track down her owners," she stated, trying to stay positive. She, Natalie and Tristan had organized the Pet Finders Club soon after Andi had moved to Aldcliffe, from Texas in America, last September. Andi had lost Buddy at the same time that Natalie had lost Jet, and the experience had made them realize how terrible it was to lose a pet. So, they'd set up the club to help other people find their missing animals.

Natalie appeared at the end of the path Andi had cleared through the shrubs. "Fisher's on his way."

"Thank goodness," Tristan said. "She looks bad." Shivering, he rubbed his bare arms, smearing mud over them.

"Here." Natalie slipped off her jacket and handed it to him. "Put this on. You look frozen."

Tristan stared at her in astonishment. "What about all this mud? I'm filthy."

Natalie's clothes always came from the most prestigious boutiques, and she always took great care of them, but she just shrugged. "That doesn't seem important now. I can always take it to the dry cleaner's."

Gratefully, Tristan slipped on the jacket. "Thanks, Nat."

"I'll wait at the top of the bank," Natalie said, "so Fisher can find us." She scrambled up the steep slope with Buddy and Jet loping beside her.

Andi went on stroking the puppy, tracing the outline of her tiny floppy ears. Did she even know Andi was there?

About ten minutes passed before Natalie began to

wave. "He's here!" she shrieked. "I can see the RSPCA ambulance!"

Andi's heart flipped over with relief. "You'll be okay now, girl," she told the puppy, crossing her fingers for luck.

Fisher appeared at the top of the bank, with a rucksack slung over his shoulder. He was a tall, dark, friendly-faced man in his early thirties. Behind him came a small, very slim woman with long brown hair tied in a ponytail. She was wearing a white tunic and matching trousers, and carrying an armful of blankets. Andi hadn't seen her before, but from her outfit it looked as though she worked at the clinic with Fisher.

"How is she?" Fisher called, jogging down the slope. He pushed the bushes aside quickly.

"Not good," Andi said. She moved aside so Fisher could take her place by the puppy's head. He knelt down and ran his hands gently over the puppy's mud-caked body.

She gave a tiny moan.

"Hang in there, girl," he murmured. "She's badly bruised," he said over his shoulder to Andi. "She might even have some broken bones and internal injuries, too. We'll have to X-ray her to be sure." He sighed.

"Poor thing. She's so young – only about twelve weeks old, I'd say."

"One of her back legs looks weird," Tristan told him, "sort of twisted."

Fisher shifted along beside the puppy and ran his hands carefully over the injured leg. The puppy didn't stir.

The woman who'd come with him slid down the bank. She set the blankets on the grass then made her way into the shrubbery. "Hi, I'm Molly," she said to Andi and Tristan. "I've just started at the clinic as a veterinary nurse. I've heard all about you Pet Finders." Andi tried to smile but she was feeling too worried about the pup. Natalie had followed Molly and stood a little way off, keeping Buddy and Jet out of the way. She looked as pale and anxious as Andi felt.

"This hip's dislocated, Molly," Fisher said. "I'll give her a painkilling injection so we can move her."

"Can you put it right?" Andi asked.

"Yes. Dislocated hips look a bit scary but they don't take long to heal. Though that doesn't necessarily mean she'll be OK, I'm afraid. There could be all sorts of other problems that we don't know about yet."

Andi felt tears well up in her eyes and swallowed

hard. *Don't give up yet, girl,* she begged silently. *You're a fighter, I know it!*

Fisher went on. "We'll take her back to the clinic and find out exactly what we're dealing with."

Molly opened a medical kit and took out a hypodermic syringe and a bottle of pale-yellowy liquid. She filled the syringe, then used a piece of lint, moistened with antiseptic, to wipe the mud from a small patch on the puppy's neck. "Here you are," she said, handing the syringe to Fisher.

For a moment after he injected the puppy nothing happened, then the young dog seemed to relax, her legs and body flattening out against the ground and her head lolling sideways.

"That's better," Fisher said. He glanced at Molly. "Let's get her wrapped up warmly. She's definitely got hypothermia."

Molly pulled a crackly metallic blanket from the pile she'd carried down the slope. She unfolded it and spread it on the ground beside the puppy. Gently, she and Fisher rolled the pup on to it, taking care not to jar her injured leg. They wrapped it round her, then Fisher picked her up carefully.

"It's lucky you found her when you did," he said as he started to make his way up the slope, cradling the tiny bundle in his arms. "I'd say she's been here for a couple of days already. Her temperature's dangerously low and I don't think she'd have lasted another night."

Andi's heart sank. She couldn't bear to think of the puppy lying here, cold and in pain, for two long days and nights. She picked up the spare blankets, Molly grabbed Fisher's medical kit, and they headed back to the pavement. Tristan squelched along behind with Natalie and the dogs.

They reached the RSPCA ambulance – a low white van with neat racks of equipment along one inside wall and a roomy cage to transport stray or injured animals on the other side. Andi flung open the back doors and Molly climbed in. Fisher laid the puppy in her lap. "I won't put her in the cage. I need you to keep checking her breathing and heartbeat."

Andi reached in and touched the muddy fur. "Just hold on, girl," she said. "You can do it!" She straightened up and Fisher shut the back door.

"I'm afraid I haven't got time to give you three a lift," he said. "But come into the clinic and visit the puppy whenever you want. That was good work, what you did for this little dog today." He smiled briefly, then raced to the driver's door, jumped in, and sped away.

The Pet Finders watched the ambulance until it

disappeared round a bend. "I hope she makes it," Tristan said shakily.

"Me too," Andi and Natalie said together.

"This isn't exactly the sort of pet-finding we're used to," Natalie said grimly. "We've never had to cope with an *injured* pet before." She handed Andi Buddy's lead. "It feels horrible. There's none of the usual energy we get with a new case."

"It was bound to happen one day," Tristan pointed out. "I mean, lost animals must be more at risk of getting knocked down on the road because they've got nobody with them to keep them safe."

Andi nodded, but she was too choked up to say anything. She hugged Buddy tight, thankful that he hadn't been injured when he was lost. Then she wished even harder for the Labrador puppy to pull through.

Chapter Two

"I wonder if anyone's reported the puppy missing?" Andi said as the Pet Finders headed for home. Tristan trudged beside them, carrying his skateboard and smelling like the bottom of a pond. "I mean, we haven't heard anything, and most people know who we are now . . ."

"I was thinking about that, too," Natalie said. "You can't exactly miss the fact that your puppy's not there any more. They're pretty noticeable!"

Andi thought back to the time when she'd first got Buddy. He'd followed her everywhere, and was endlessly setting little tokens at her feet – her mum's shoes, newspapers, cushions . . . Once he even dug up a small rose bush and dragged it indoors. "Yes," she agreed. "You'd definitely notice if your puppy disappeared."

"I think she's been dumped," Tristan said gloomily.

Andi and Natalie stopped walking. "No!" Andi exclaimed. "That's too cruel!"

Natalie shook her head. "You're wrong, Tris. Puppies are adorable – especially Labrador puppies." She bent down to hug Jet and he licked her nose. "Nobody could be that horrible."

"She was on the busiest road in Aldcliffe." Tristan shifted his skateboard to the other arm, releasing another whiff of pond. "Dogs don't like traffic, so even if she was lost, she'd have turned back when she came to this road." He set his mouth in a straight line.

"I think you're wrong about this, Tris," Natalie argued.

Andi frowned. What Tristan said made sense, but she couldn't believe that anyone would be cruel enough to abandon a young puppy on a busy main road.

"If she's only lost, then why hasn't her owner reported her missing?" Tristan pointed out. "Fisher and Molly didn't say anything about a missing Labrador puppy, so nobody can have phoned the RSPCA either."

"Perhaps her owner didn't think of ringing there,"

Natalie said. "Perhaps they phoned the police instead. We should ring them to find out."

"Good idea," Andi agreed.

The Pet Finders cut across the park. Red and white tulips marched along the edge of the grass and the trees rustled their new leaves. The sun was just dipping behind the mountains on the horizon and the shadows were lengthening.

Andi let Buddy off his lead. He went tearing away, then circled back as though they were a flock of sheep to be rounded up. She envied him for being happy when she couldn't stop thinking about the poor puppy.

Jet looked hopefully at Natalie. "Sorry, Jet!" she said, "but I am *not* letting you off your lead. You wouldn't stay with us like Buddy does." She released the catch on his extendable lead and he trotted away while the lead unreeled behind him. A few ducks swam towards them, quacking for bread, when they reached the pond in the middle of the park. Buddy raced to the water's edge and barked, his stumpy little tail stuck straight out behind him.

"Do you think it would be OK to ring Fisher as soon as we get home, to find out how the puppy's doing?" Andi asked.

"Not straight away," Tristan warned. "We don't want to interrupt him or Molly treating the puppy. One of us should phone the police, though, like Natalie said."

"I'll do it," Andi offered.

"Let us know what they say," Natalie said. "If they don't know anything about her, we should start searching for her owner. After all, we've found stray pets before, haven't we?" Andi was reminded of Apple, the Border terrier they'd first spotted running across the park a few months earlier.

They reached a narrow path that led out to the road. Andi clipped on Buddy's lead. 'I'll ring you later,' she promised Natalie and Tristan. As she jogged away with Buddy scampering beside her, she tried to feel more positive about the injured puppy. They'd found lost owners before – why not aim for another happy reunion?

Andi's mum, Judy Talbot, was cooking dinner when she got home, and the house smelt delicious. "Hello, darling. Had a good walk?" she asked, pulling some potatoes from a carrier bag.

"Not exactly," Andi called back. "Stay, Bud." Buddy sat down obediently on the doormat and watched Andi as she hung up her muddy jacket and grabbed his special towel from the hall cupboard.

"What happened?" Mrs Talbot asked, appearing in the kitchen doorway with a half-peeled potato in her hand.

Andi started to dry Buddy's muddy paws; he made it tricky by catching the towel in his teeth and trying to yank it away from her. She told her mum about the injured puppy. "Fisher's trying to make her better now," she said. Her voice shook. "Oh, Mum, I'm not sure she's going to make it."

Her mum came over and gave her a hug. "That poor little puppy! Still, it sounds as though she's a fighter. She's held on until now, so she must be strong."

"I wish we'd found her earlier."

"It's lucky you found her at all, darling. Good for Tris, falling off his skateboard in exactly the right place!"

Andi nodded. She'd thought about that on her way home. If Tristan hadn't wanted to practise skateboard jumps, if he hadn't fallen into the ditch, if Buddy hadn't found the puppy . . . She shivered. "Can I phone the police and see if anyone's reported her missing?"

"Of course you can." Mrs Talbot let her go, then gave her an encouraging smile. "Are you okay, now?"

Andi smiled back. "Yeah, thanks."

"In that case, I'll be in the kitchen if you need me."

Andi dialled the number of the police station. A policeman answered on the third ring.

"Hello. My name's Andi Talbot. My friends and I found an injured puppy near the main road out of Aldcliffe earlier today," she explained. "It's a Labrador. Has anyone reported losing one?"

"Just a minute, Andi, I'll check the lost-pet register."

Andi heard him flicking through pages, then he spoke again: "Sorry, no one's lost a Labrador puppy. Have you called the RSPCA?"

"Yes, she's there already," Andi told him. "We called Fisher Pearce, who's a friend of ours, and he picked her up in the ambulance."

"It sounds as though you've done this before," the policeman said, sounding impressed.

"Yes. My friends and I are the Pet Finders Club. We track down lost pets – or, sometimes, lost owners."

"I've heard about you," the policeman said. "You found the animals that were stolen from Paws for Thought, didn't you?"

"That's right," Andi said. "But nobody's phoned us about losing a Labrador puppy."

"Give me your phone number," the policeman said.

"I'll give you a ring if I hear anything. And if you need to phone us again, ask for me. I'm Sergeant Poole."

Andi gave him her number. "Thanks for your help." Just as she hung up the phone, it rang again. She snatched it up, hoping it was information about the Labrador. "Hello?"

"Is this the Pet Finders Club?" asked a woman's voice.

"Yes! Can I help you?" Andi picked up the pen that lay beside the phone.

"My name's Mrs Jupp. My son's guinea pig, Cocoa, has disappeared."

Andi felt a twinge of disappointment that the call wasn't about the puppy. Still, it would be good to have another case to work on, too. "Okay. We'll need to take some details." She wrote down the woman's name and address. "We can come over in about half an hour, if that's any good for you." Fisher had Natalie's mobile phone number, so they wouldn't need to stay at home waiting for news of the puppy.

When Mrs Jupp said that would be fine, Andi phoned Tristan and Natalie to tell them about the missing guinea pig, then went into the kitchen. Her mum was chopping carrots. "Any news?"

"No. Someone's lost a guinea pig. I've got to go out again. What time's dinner?"

Her mum glanced at the clock. "Not for another hour and a half."

"Okay. I'm only going to Cooper's Hill. Natalie and Tristan are meeting me there. I'll take Rachel's bike so I'll be extra-fast." Rachel Brand, the owner of a corner shop near Andi's house, had lent Andi a top-of-the-range mountain bike so she could keep up with Natalie and Tristan.

Buddy darted into the hall as Andi grabbed her coat. "Not this time, Bud," she said. "I'm not sure you'd be very helpful on a guinea pig hunt." She patted him, then pelted out of the front door, leaving him gazing mournfully after her.

The sun was setting in a blaze of crimson and pink as Andi pedalled up Cooper's Hill. Mrs Jupp's house stood near the top, and Andi grinned to herself. On another one of their recent cases, a missing Dalmatian named Raisin had had owners who lived at the top of a hill. Natalie wasn't into sports like Andi was, and she'd complained bitterly about trekking up and down the hill to speak to Mr and Mrs Harris on a regular basis.

The Jupps' house was faced with white weatherboarding. Shutters hung on either side of the windows. There was a kid's bike lying in the front garden. Andi was the first to arrive, but Tristan and Natalie weren't far behind her. Tristan had obviously had a shower and changed his clothes; there wasn't a trace of mud on him now.

"Any news of the puppy?" Andi asked at once.

"Not yet,' Natalie said. "Have you phoned the police?"

"Yes, but they didn't know anything."

"Told you she'd been dumped," Tristan said darkly.

Natalie sighed. "You don't know what you're talking about, Tristan. There's no way—"

"Whoa, hold on!" Andi interrupted. "We're here to find a lost guinea pig, not to argue about what might have happened to the puppy."

As they walked up Mrs Jupp's driveway, the front door opened and a dark-haired boy aged about six came out on to the porch. "Are you the Pet Finders Club?"

"Yep," Andi replied. "Is your mum in?"

A tall woman appeared behind the boy. "Hello! Come in," she said, smiling warmly. "I'm Mrs Jupp."

"I'm Tristan Saunders," Tristan said, as they

followed her along a wide hall. "And these are the other Pet Finders, Andi Talbot and Natalie Lewis."

"Pleased to meet you." Mrs Jupp showed them into a living room cluttered with toys. "It was nice of you to come so quickly."

"So, what happened?" Natalie asked. "If we know how your guinea pig was lost, it might help us work out where she is."

"It was Shane who found her missing," Mrs Jupp replied. "Tell them what happened, darling."

"Cocoa was in her hutch in the garden with her friend, Sugar," the little boy tried to explain, his forehead creasing with worry. "When I went out to feed them, Sugar was there, but Cocoa wasn't."

"Had the door of the hutch come open?" asked Andi.

Shane shook his head. "No, it was shut. I don't know how she got out."

Tristan took notes in the red notebook he used for every case. "When did you notice she was missing?"

"Just before Mum phoned you. We came back from shopping. Mum said we should ring because it's such a mystery how she got out."

"Can we see the hutch?" Natalie suggested.

Mrs Jupp opened a pair of French doors at the back

of the living room, and they went out into a small garden. The sun had almost gone now and the garden was full of deep shadows. A neat wooden hutch stood at the end of the lawn, next to a shed. A white guinea pig was sitting inside the hutch, nibbling hay. A path led past the hutch to a gate at the bottom of the garden.

"The guinea pigs live outside in spring and summer," Mrs Jupp explained. "They love sunbathing."

"Perhaps the hinge is broken on the door of the hutch," Andi whispered, remembering how Lola, a valuable Russian Blue cat, had escaped from her owner's home.

Tristan nodded. "Like Lola, you mean?" he said, reading her mind. "Good idea. Let's check."

"Hello. You must be Sugar. Aren't you sweet?" Natalie said to the guinea pig as she unbolted the door. The guinea pig gazed up at her, its nose twitching.

"Don't be scared, Sugar," Shane said, crouching beside the hutch. "They're here to find Cocoa."

The guinea pig gave a high-pitched squeak before scampering into its sleeping compartment.

Tristan laughed. "I always thought you looked scary, Nat."

Natalie made a face at him, then examined the door. "The hinges are fine," she announced. "And the wire mesh is tight. There's no way Cocoa could have got through here."

"Unless the door wasn't closed properly," Andi said. She rattled the bolt, but it fitted well and slid easily into place. As she checked the door to the sleeping compartment, Sugar dashed back into the main part of her hutch. "This door's okay, too." She reached into the hutch very slowly and stroked the guinea pig with one finger, trying to calm her. "It's okay, girl, we won't hurt you."

"Do Sugar and Cocoa look alike, Mrs Jupp?" Tristan asked.

"Oh, no. Cocoa's chocolate-brown."

"I've got a picture of her by my bed," Shane said. 'Do you want to see it?"

"That would be great!" Tristan agreed.

Shane hurried inside.

Andi and Natalie closed the hutch, checking that the bolt was securely in place, then went to examine the back gate. It wasn't locked, and Tristan opened it to reveal a narrow alleyway that ran behind all the houses in the road. The gate had no gaps around it, so the guinea pig couldn't have escaped that way.

Tristan drew a quick sketch of the gate in his notebook.

"Honestly, Tris, we all know what a gate looks like!" Natalie exclaimed.

He grinned sheepishly and crossed it out. "Yeah. I suppose so."

Shane came back, clutching the photo. "This is her."

Andi took the photo, which was in a red and green frame. "She looks really cute. Do you think we could keep this for a little while? We need to scan it into my computer and make posters so everyone will know to look out for Cocoa."

Shane bit his lip. "You won't lose it, will you? It's the only one I've got." He looked as though he was about to cry. "Sugar is lovely," he added, "but Cocoa's my real favourite."

"We'll be really careful with it," Andi promised. "Look, Tristan's got a special wallet for photos in his notebook."

Tristan slid the photo out of the frame and put it inside the clear plastic pouch. "It'll be safe there."

Shane looked a bit happier as he took back the empty frame. "Are you going to make the posters now?"

"It'll have to be tomorrow. It's getting late," Andi

replied. "And we need to search for Cocoa in your garden, but it's too dark now."

"We've already searched our garden," Mrs Jupp said. "She's definitely not here."

Andi frowned. "I don't see how she could have got right out of the garden."

"Well, actually, the gate was open," said Shane.

"Are you sure, darling?" asked Mrs Jupp, looking surprised. "You didn't mention it before."

The little boy opened his eyes very wide. "I just remembered, but it *was* open."

"So she might have gone out into the alley," Tristan said. He lowered his voice. "Do you think someone came in through the gate and stole her?"

"Maybe," Natalie replied. "But it would be pretty mean to steal a little kid's pet. It's more likely she's just wandered out of the garden."

"You *are* going to find her, aren't you?" Shane's voice quivered.

Andi smiled, trying to reassure him. "We'll do everything we can. Don't worry – we haven't been beaten yet!" All the same, she couldn't help feeling anxious: there were so many dangers facing a little lost guinea pig. She hoped Cocoa would find somewhere safe to hide.

Chapter Three

The next day after school, the Pet Finders hurried to the RSPCA. Fisher was sitting in the reception area, sorting out a pile of forms.

"How's the puppy?" Andi asked, straight away. Fisher had called Natalie on her mobile phone the night before to say that the pup was still alive, but Andi had hardly been able to concentrate at school, wondering constantly how she was doing.

Fisher stood up and smiled. "She's going to be fine! We've X-rayed her and, luckily, she hasn't got any broken bones or internal injuries."

"What about the hypothermia?" Natalie wanted to know.

"Her temperature's back to normal, thanks to a warm drip. Molly took it out about fifteen minutes ago."

"And her dislocated hip?" said Tristan.

"It's back in place. She's still a bit dopey from the anaesthetic, but that's a good thing because she needs to rest. Apart from that, she's bruised and she's got a couple of minor cuts. She'll be a bit stiff and sore for a few days, but she'll make a full recovery."

Andi high-fived Natalie and Tristan. The puppy was going to get better! It was the best news ever! 'Can we see her?"

"Of course you can," Fisher said. 'I'll take you through." He led them into a large room filled with pens and cages of different sizes. Molly was scrubbing down a counter at the far end of the room, but she looked round and smiled at them.

"Hello! Did Fisher tell you the good news?"

The Pet Finders grinned back. "You bet!" Tristan exclaimed. 'And it's—" He broke off and his eyes stretched wide with delight. "Wow! Look at these geckos!" He darted to a cage containing a pair of green geckos and a branch for them to climb on. The geckos gazed at him, their yellow eyes unblinking and their tongues flicking in and out.

"Trust you to make a beeline for them," Natalie said. She crouched down beside a cage with a low wooden hutch at one end. "These are much cuter."

There were five fluffy, white baby rabbits scampering about in the sawdust. A bigger rabbit – the babies' mother, Andi guessed – was nibbling a carrot, but she stopped chewing and sat up on her hind legs as they bent down. One of the babies came cautiously to the wire, its pink nose snuffling. Andi pushed her fingers through and stroked its downy fur.

Suddenly they heard a high-pitched shout. "Ahoy there!" The baby rabbits skittered back to their mother.

"What was that?" Andi gasped.

Fisher laughed. "It's only Captain." He pointed to a green-and-red parrot that was strutting along its perch in a tall cage. "Time for lunch! Lovely!" it screeched. 'Lovely! Lovely!"

The Pet Finders laughed. "He's almost as loud as Long John Silver," Natalie said.

"Who?" Molly looked puzzled.

"Fisher's mum and dad have got a parrot," Andi explained. "They own the Banana Beach Café in the high street. Long John Silver seems to spend most of his time squawking about bananas."

Molly grinned. "I look forward to meeting him."

"Are all these animals lost?" Tristan asked. From the way he said it, Andi knew he was hoping Fisher would let them track down the owners.

Fisher shook his head. "No, the rabbits were left on our doorstep one night. The geckos' owner found that looking after them was too much trouble. And Captain's owner was an old lady who's gone to live in a home. None of them will be here long. We'll find new homes for them. We've already placed two cats and a hamster this month."

Tristan looked longingly at the geckos. "Can anyone have them?"

"No. We check prospective owners out first, to make sure they're responsible."

"That rules you out, Tris," Natalie whispered.

"Thanks," Tristan said in mock indignation.

"You've got Lucy to look after now, anyway," Andi added. "You'd never have time for geckos, too." Tristan's cat Lucy had been missing for months until the Pet Finders had recently tracked her down.

Tristan beamed at her. "You don't have to remind me. Having Lucy home is fantastic!"

"The puppy's through here," Fisher said. He led them to a door at the end of the room. "This is the intensive-treatment room. She should be well enough to move into the main room tomorrow."

The cages in the intensive-treatment room were smaller, and only one was occupied. The Pet Finders

crowded round. The puppy was lying inside on a white blanket. She was a lot cleaner than she had been when they found her, though streaks of dried mud still clung to her fur.

"She's a *golden* Labrador!" Tristan exclaimed. "She was so muddy yesterday it was impossible to tell."

"She wasn't the only one!" Natalie grinned at Tristan.

The puppy had a small cut on one leg, and another just below her ear, but they obviously didn't bother her too much: her tail began to wag the moment she saw the Pet Finders and she struggled into a sitting position.

"Hello, girl!" Andi whispered. Her heart was zinging with happiness. Only yesterday, she'd been afraid the puppy wouldn't last the night; now she seemed to be making a miraculous recovery. And she was *so* gorgeous! She pushed her fingers through the mesh of the cage and the puppy licked them.

"We should think of a name for her," Natalie suggested. "You know, like we called that Border terrier Oat until we found out her real name was Apple. We can't keep calling her *the puppy*." She frowned thoughtfully. 'How about Goldie?"

"Not very original," Andi pointed out. "After

everything she's been through, she needs an extra-special name." She rubbed the side of the pup's head, trying to think of a name to suit her, but nothing seemed right.

"We'll have to hurry up and find her owner now," Natalie said, reaching in to run a velvety ear through her fingers. "They must be so worried about her."

"Absolutely," Fisher agreed. "But I'm sure you Pet Finders will find out where she's from."

"I think she's been dumped," Tristan said. "Could she have been pushed out of a moving car, do you think?"

Andi gasped. "Oh, no! Nobody could have done that to her, Tris!"

Fisher shook his head. "No. She's only bruised on one side of her body and that must have happened when she was hit by a car. Luckily it was only a light blow. If she'd been pushed out of a moving car, I think she'd have been much more badly hurt. I'd expect to find two distinct areas of bruising, one from the fall and the other from the impact with the car."

Andi was relieved that Tristan's theory seemed to be wrong but, all the same, she shivered. She could imagine the little dog's terror as she went bowling down the steep bank, knocked off her paws by a passing vehicle.

"If she hasn't been dumped, why hasn't anybody reported her missing?" Tristan persisted. "And why was she on that busy road at all? She wouldn't have gone there by herself with all that traffic rushing past."

"It does look a bit odd," Fisher agreed, "but it's not cut and dried. It's important to find the puppy's owner, but we need to be a bit wary. We don't want her going home to someone who's not fit to look after her. On the other hand, perhaps there's an innocent explanation for everything."

Andi's head was reeling. She still couldn't understand why anyone would abandon such a cute puppy. But if she hadn't been dumped, why hadn't anyone reported her missing? Andi felt torn in two directions at once. All she knew for sure was that the puppy needed their help, and the Pet Finders were going to have to do everything they could to make sure she ended up with someone who really cared about her.

Chapter Four

"Let's make Cocoa's posters first," Andi suggested, sitting down at the computer in her mum's study. Buddy flopped down under the desk and rested his head on her feet. "We've got everything we need for those," she continued. "We haven't got a photo of the puppy yet, and it might be better to wait until her cuts have healed a bit before we start taking pictures of her."

"And the puppy's safe at the RSPCA," Tristan pointed out. "But the guinea pig's in danger while she's on the loose." He perched on the edge of the desk and took the red notebook out of his rucksack. Removing Cocoa's photo from the pouch, he handed it to Andi. "Here you are."

She scanned it into the computer, then typed LOST underneath, to begin with.

"We can ask people to look under bushes and in sheds," Tristan said. "And they should check under parked cars and—"

"OK, OK, slow down!" Andi exclaimed. "I'm not *that* fast at typing."

The poster was soon finished. Andi printed off a trial copy and passed it round. "What do you think?"

"Not bad," Tristan said approvingly. "Let's hope it works. I hate to think of Cocoa scampering around all alone." Andi set the computer to print twenty more copies, then she reduced the size of the poster and printed another thirty flyers to put through letter-boxes in the Jupps' road.

Andi glanced out of the window and saw that it was raining. "We should meet up in the morning and put these up before school," she suggested.

"Uh, what time in the morning?" Natalie asked suspiciously.

"Seven o'clock."

"Seven o'clock? No thanks!"

"You've got to come, Nat. We're the Pet Finders; we do stuff together. And this case is urgent."

"Yeah, but – *seven* o'clock?"

"And we should jog there," Andi continued, "so we can get fit at the same time."

41

"Jog!" Natalie sank back into her chair. "You're off your head."

"Completely insane," Tristan agreed.

"It's athletics season," Andi reminded them. "I should be jogging every day." Andi loved athletics, and try-outs were coming up for the school team.

"Can't we use our bikes?" Natalie said. "Tristan could come on his skateboard."

Tristan frowned. "Actually, I can't. One of the bearings broke when I fell off the other day." He dropped the red notebook into his rucksack and stood up. "And I can't borrow Dean's because he'll be delivering his papers. I hate to say it, but I think Andi's right. We *will* have to jog. Worse luck!"

"We'll meet outside the school. Don't forget to wear your trainers, Nat," Andi said, giving her friend a playful jab on her arm.

Natalie groaned and waved Andi away with her hand.

"Well, I'd better go home," Tristan said. "I've got a pile of homework the size of Mount Everest."

"I can't believe we're going to do this," Natalie said as she followed Tristan downstairs. "I mean – jogging! And at seven o'clock in the morning."

Andi laughed. "See you then," she said, as Tristan

and Natalie put up their hoods and went out into the rain.

The next morning, the sun was shining and the sky was clear blue. Andi jogged to Fairfield Middle School with Buddy scampering happily beside her: there was nothing he liked better than an early run.

Tristan was already there. "Do you think Nat will turn up?"

Andi looked along the street. "Here she comes now. And she's brought Jet."

Natalie was pounding determinedly along the pavement, wearing a spotless white T-shirt, pink Lycra shorts, and silver trainers that gleamed in the early-morning sunshine. "Typical," Andi said, as Natalie reached them.

Buddy and Jet touched noses, then danced around each other. Jet began to bark. "We'd better go," Andi said. "We've got to leave enough time to get home again before school, and we don't want Jet waking people up. It's a bit early."

"You can say that again," Natalie muttered.

They set off, jogging. At first, Tristan tried to keep pace with Andi, while Natalie puffed along behind. Soon he fell back and, by the time they reached the end of the road, quite a gap had opened up between them. Andi waited for them to catch up. "Come on!" she called, running on the spot.

"I don't know why I came," Natalie panted when she reached Andi. "I knew this would be a disaster." She hunched over with her hands on her knees. Jet leapt around her, pulling on his lead. "Stop it, Jet!" she groaned. "It's too early to play."

"Next time I mention jogging," Tristan puffed, sinking down on a garden wall, "would someone please remind me that I'm a natural couch potato?"

"Think of all the good it's doing you," Andi said, but she could tell neither of them was convinced. "And think of poor Cocoa."

"I know, I know," Natalie said, still breathless, "but I just need a minute to get my breath back."

"I'll go on ahead, or we won't have time to put any of these posters up," Andi said, and she set off at a sprint.

"Slow down!" Natalie wailed.

Cooper's Hill was hardly any distance away but by the time Andi reached the corner, Tristan and Natalie were a long way behind. "I don't know, Bud," she laughed, stooping down to stroke him. "These people who never get any exercise!" She took the posters out of her rucksack and tied one to a tree. Cocoa's cute face stared back at her. "I hope these do the trick," she said aloud.

Tristan and Natalie arrived at last, red-faced and out of breath. Andi divided up the pile of posters and flyers and handed them out, keeping one poster for the school notice board and another to hang in the window of Paws for Thought, the pet shop owned by Christine Wilson.

"Here," Andi said. "If we get a move on, there should just be time for a quick search along the Jupps' road before we have to head back."

Natalie glanced at the steep hill ahead of them and shuddered.

"It's OK," Andi said. "Bud and I will go up the hill. You and Tris can start down here."

Soon every tree and lamppost on Cooper's Hill, and the roads around it, displayed a lost guinea pig poster, and a flyer had been pushed through every letterbox. The Pet Finders met halfway up the hill. Tristan and Natalie had recovered from their run now, though Natalie's face was still red and shiny.

"Let's start searching in the alley behind the Jupps' house," Tristan suggested. "That's the most likely place for Cocoa to be. She could have escaped through the

back gate. And she'd try to keep herself hidden in case there were any predators about."

They found a narrow passageway between two houses that looked as though it might lead into the alley. It was obviously not used much; they had to push their way through tall weeds and drooping branches that hung over from the gardens on either side. They searched among the weeds carefully – it was just the sort of place a lost and frightened guinea pig might hide – but they reached the alley without seeing any sign of Cocoa.

The alley ran straight in both directions. It was rutted and stony, with tufts of coarse grass. Several houses had garages here, and a few dustbins stood beside back gates.

"Let's head up the hill towards the Jupps'," Natalie suggested. They turned left and continued their search, standing on tiptoe to look over fences, peering behind dustbins and into clumps of thick grass.

"We should look for gnawed places on fences, too," Tristan said. "Guinea pigs nibble wood to stop their teeth getting too long, so if we found bite marks we'd know Cocoa had been along here."

Just before they reached the Jupps' house, Andi

glanced at her watch. It was quarter past eight. "We'd better stop. We'll be late for school."

As they headed back down the alley, Tristan sighed. "Guinea pigs are so small and vulnerable . . ." He didn't finish, but Andi knew exactly what he meant: Cocoa would be no match for a hungry cat or fox. The thought made her shiver. They had to find the guinea pig quickly. If it wasn't already too late . . .

Chapter Five

The Pet Finders walked down to the RSPCA after school to visit the Labrador puppy. Molly was sitting in the reception area. She was holding a milk dropper in one hand and a pink, featherless baby bird in the other. Its beak kept opening and shutting and it was chirping loudly.

The Pet Finders crept closer, not wanting to frighten it. "Where did you get the baby bird?" Andi whispered.

Molly dripped milk into the tiny beak. "Someone brought it in. It fell out of its nest."

"How's the dog with no name?" Natalie asked.

"See for yourself!" Smiling, Molly set down the dropper and, ignoring the baby bird's insistent chirps, opened the door that led into the animal unit. The puppy was curled up in a cage near the door. She lifted her head as they approached, then pushed herself to her paws. They all bent down and reached through the mesh. The puppy licked their fingers, her tail wagging the tiniest bit.

"She's still a bit muddy, I'm afraid," Molly said. "I've been trying to find time to bath her all day, but it's been really hectic here."

"Can we let her out?" said Natalie.

"Yes, though I don't think she'll feel much like running. She's still quite stiff."

"Her cuts look as though they're healing up," Tristan remarked.

"They are. Her temperature's normal, too, and that hip's as good as new."

The Pet Finders opened the cage door. The puppy came towards them slowly, her tail twitching from side to side. "Hello, girl. How are you feeling?" Andi murmured, bending down to stroke her.

When Tristan sat cross-legged on the floor, the puppy crawled on to his lap and snuggled down. Now they could see the flecks of dried mud still caught in her fur.

"She's so gorgeous," Natalie said, smoothing the sunshine-yellow fur on the top of the pup's head. "We really can't keep on calling her 'the dog with no name'. We've got to think of a temporary name for her."

"It's so difficult," Andi said. "There are loads of names that would fit her. How can we pick the right one?"

They sat silent for a few moments, thinking hard. "I give up. Let's think about something else," Tristan said. 'You know, Molly said she hasn't had time to give her a bath? Well, why don't *we* do it?"

"Do you think they'll let us?" Natalie asked eagerly.

"Only one way to find out." Andi stood up and went back to reception with Natalie. The baby bird was asleep, lying in a plastic bowl lined with newspaper. It didn't look as comfy as a nest, but it was a lot safer than being on a pavement. Molly was washing her hands in a sink at the far end of the room.

"We were wondering if we could bath the puppy," Andi said. "We'll be really careful with her."

Molly smiled over her shoulder. "That would be a big help. I'll give you a hand to fill the bath." She got a shallow plastic bathtub out of a walk-in cupboard and carried it to the sink. Andi squirted a dollop of dog shampoo into the tub and turned on the tap. The shampoo began to foam.

"That should do it," Molly said, when the bath was

51

half-full. She tested the temperature of the water with her hand. "Perfect. Can you two manage the bath? I'll bring a towel."

Andi and Natalie carefully lifted the heavy bathtub together, shuffling with small side-steps back to the doors of the animal unit, where Tristan let them in. The bubbles shimmered with rainbows of colour as they set the bath down. The puppy looked up and sniffed the air, her round black nose quivering. Then she stood up on Tristan's lap and stretched gingerly.

"Come on, girl!" Andi called. "Bath time."

The puppy padded towards her, her thick soft ears pricked up and her brown eyes bright. Tristan followed her.

"You'll have to ruffle her fur a bit to get at the mud on her skin," Molly said. She handed the white fluffy towel to Natalie. "Labradors have two layers of hair and the under coat is waterproof."

"Waterproof?" Natalie echoed. "Why would a dog need a waterproof coat?"

"Labradors are good swimmers," Molly explained. "Fishermen in Newfoundland in Canada used to keep Labs to help them drag their nets out of the water."

"That must be how she stayed warm enough to survive when she fell in the ditch," Andi said thoughtfully.

"Well, I'll leave you to it," said Molly. "Shout if you need me."

"Is it OK to lift her?" Natalie checked. "We don't want to hurt her."

"I'm sure you'll be gentle," Molly replied. "Just don't rub too hard when you're washing her."

"Do you think she likes baths?" Natalie wondered, when Molly had gone. "Jet is terrible. He always plays up."

"Buddy loves being bathed," Andi said. "Let's hope this puppy's more like him." She lifted the pup carefully and set her down in the warm water. The little Labrador looked down at the foam for a moment, then flopped down so that only her head was above the water. The bubbles around her neck made it look as though she was wearing a lacy ruff.

"Good girl!" Andi laughed. She scooped up a handful of water and let it trickle over the puppy's fluffy ears. The little Labrador gave a tiny yap, as if to tell them to do it again.

"She loves this," Tristan said, crouching down to rub her back.

The puppy dipped her nose into the bubbles and sneezed. She stared round at the Pet Finders, wide-eyed with surprise. They all laughed and the puppy's tail wagged harder, flicking bubbles over them. "You're right, Tris," Andi agreed. "She *does* like it!"

Andi and Tristan washed the puppy carefully, working the soap bubbles through her fur to clean away the last of the mud, while Natalie spread the towel over her lap, ready to dry her. "We still haven't thought of a name for her," she reminded them.

"I've got one," Tristan said with a grin. "How about Fang?"

"Fang!" Natalie hooted. "Does this sweet little dog look like a Fang? And, in any case, her owners would never have called her a name like that."

"How about Ripper, then?" Tristan suggested. "If she has a really tough-sounding name, she'll be able to stick up for herself if other dogs try to bully her."

"Yeah, as though that would work!" Natalie retorted.

"Demon?" Tristan said. "Or Gnasher or—"

"OK, Tris," Andi interrupted. "Don't get carried away." She wiped bubbles from the puppy's head. "You don't want a fierce name, do you, girl?"

The puppy twisted her head and licked Andi's hand. "There's your answer, Tris," Andi joked. "She doesn't think much of your ideas. And neither do we."

"You're only saying that because you didn't think of them yourself," Tristan said, pretending to be offended. "Fang's a great name. We could get her a studded collar and—"

"No we couldn't!" Andi and Natalie said together.

"I think we're pretty well finished here," Andi said. "Out you come, girl." She lifted the pup out of the bath and set her on Natalie's lap. Natalie wrapped her in the towel and patted her gently. The dog leant against her chest, grunting with pleasure.

Andi and Tristan hauled the bathtub back to the sink and emptied it. Andi rinsed it and wiped it dry, then returned it to the cupboard. By the time they got back, Natalie had finished drying the puppy. Her damp fur stood up in golden spikes all over her body.

"That's better," Natalie said, and set her down on the floor. She tried to smooth down her fur. "Maybe we should call her Spike."

"Too boyish," Andi said, wrinkling her nose.

The puppy walked in a rather wobbly circle. "She

doesn't look so stiff any more," Tristan said. "That warm water must have helped with her aches and pains."

Andi shook out the puppy's blanket and refolded it to get rid of any uncomfortable creases. "There you are, girl."

The puppy padded into the cage, then settled down in her basket with her head on her paws. In a few moments she was fast asleep – it seemed that having a bath was tiring work.

"We should go," Natalie said. "We've still got to find Shane's guinea pig, and we need to work on finding the puppy's owners."

Fisher came into the room. "Hello, you three," he said. "The puppy's looking good, isn't she?"

"Great!" Tristan agreed. "Can we bring her a bone as a treat?"

"Actually, bones are too hard for her teeth yet. She's only about twelve weeks old."

"How about corn?" Andi suggested. "Corn on the cob, I mean. Buddy loved it when he was little."

"Corncobs?" queried Natalie.

"That's a good idea, Andi," Fisher said enthusiastically. "I've never heard of a dog eating corncobs, but it sounds perfect. Crunchy for puppy teeth, but soft enough for young gums."

"So it's OK if we come and see her again?" Tristan said.

"Of course. Anyone can visit. The more contact she has with people, the more social skills she'll learn. We don't want her to turn into a loner when she's still so young. It'll stop her getting bored, too, if she has plenty of visitors."

The Pet Finders went out into the sunshine. "Let's get Buddy and Jet and go down to Paws for Thought," Tristan suggested. "We can ask Christine if she knows of anyone who's lost a Labrador puppy or found a missing guinea pig. We mustn't forget we've got two cases to solve."

As the Pet Finders headed for Paws for Thought with Buddy and Jet trotting beside them, they heard the sound of rapid footsteps. A moment later, Mike Morgan, the postman, came sprinting around the corner. He was tall and lean with black dreadlocked hair tied back in a ponytail.

Jet raced over to say hello, his extendable lead unreeling and his tail wagging furiously. Buddy ran close behind, yanking Andi after him. The postman staggered back with a startled yell.

"Don't worry, Mike!" said Andi, pulling Jet and Buddy back.

"O – OK." Mike eyed the dogs anxiously.

Andi noticed that his hand was bandaged. "What's happened to your hand?"

"A German Shepherd bit me last week." He shook his head. "I didn't see it until I was halfway up the driveway with a parcel, but it had been lying down in the shade. Chased me all the way to the gate! I'd have got away, too, if the catch on the gate hadn't been so stiff." He sighed melodramatically. "Dogs just *do not* like postmen!"

"Not all of them," Natalie said. "Jet's friendly to everyone!"

"So's Buddy," Andi added.

"I won't test them on that, if you don't mind." Mike edged away from the dogs as he spoke, then took a parcel out of his bag and looked down at it, his forehead creasing in a frown.

"Is everything OK?" asked Tristan.

Mike shrugged. "I suppose so. It's just that I've got this box to deliver." He glanced nervously across the road. "There's a really big dog at this address. I haven't seen it, but it always barks when I ring the doorbell. I try to put all the post through the letterbox, but this box is too big. I'll have to take it to the door and, with my luck, the dog will burst out the moment someone answers the bell."

"I'll take it," Andi offered.

The lines in Mike's face smoothed out. "Really?"

"Of course. I don't mind big dogs."

Mike handed her the parcel, holding it at arm's length, so that Buddy couldn't get too near him. "It's number three, just over there." He pointed to a bungalow with a birdbath in the middle of the front lawn.

Andi checked that no cars were coming, then ran across the road and up the driveway. Buddy scampered beside her, his claws clicking on the path. As soon as she pressed the doorbell, a dog inside began to bark. It sounded enormous. Buddy pricked up his ears and put his front paws on the doorstep, ready to make friends. Andi held his lead tightly: she didn't want him diving inside when the door opened – strange dogs could be unpredictable.

To Andi's astonishment, a tiny old lady opened the door. Andi couldn't imagine how she could possibly look after such a big dog; it was a wonder it didn't pull her over when she took it for walks. "Hello, dear," the lady said.

"I've got a parcel for you," Andi explained, handing it over. She peered past the lady, hoping to catch a glimpse of her pet. "Your dog sounds huge."

The lady winked at Andi. She had a very sweet face and twinkling blue eyes. "That's not a dog, dear. It's a tape recording. It switches on automatically when someone presses the doorbell. Don't tell anyone, will you? I feel better with people thinking there's a big fierce dog living here!"

Andi laughed. "It's scaring away the postman! Can I tell *him*?"

She thought about it for a moment and then said, "I don't see why not."

Andi crossed back over the road and told Mike what she had learnt.

"A recording?" He tutted indignantly. "Honestly! I've been dreading delivering that parcel, and all the time there wasn't a thing to worry about!" He thanked Andi, said goodbye to the others and jogged away, shaking his head.

Christine's cocker spaniel, Max, was lying in his favourite sunny spot in the pet shop window. He stood up, wagging his tail, and trotted over to greet them. Andi ran her hand over his silky fur. "Hi, boy!"

Max touched noses with Buddy and Jet.

Christine came out of the storeroom behind the shop. "Hello there! I thought I heard voices." She had dark curly hair that hung to her shoulders, and she was wearing jeans and a dark-green sweatshirt with the Paws for Thought logo – a dog's paw print surrounded by the name of the shop – printed on the front. "I hear you saved a puppy yesterday."

"You've been talking to Fisher," Tristan deduced.

Christine grinned and held up her hands. "You got me! He popped in yesterday evening."

"We thought you might know the puppy's owner," Natalie said. "The puppy's a golden Labrador, about twelve weeks old."

Christine shook her head. "I know plenty of people with golden Labs, but none as young as that. Still, I'll ask around. Do you want me to put up a poster for her?"

"We haven't made one yet," Andi admitted. "We thought we'd wait until her cuts healed before we take her picture. But we *have* got a guinea pig poster. Would you mind if we put that up?"

"A lost guinea pig?" Christine said, as Natalie stuck the poster in the window. "Have you got any clues to investigate?"

"Not really," Tristan confessed. "Has anyone tried to sell you a guinea pig lately?"

"No."

"Or maybe you've had a new customer who's bought guinea pig food or a book about guinea pigs?"

"No, sorry." She stopped as a thin-faced man came in, carrying a large dog basket. "Hang on a minute," she said. "I need to serve this man."

"Hello," he greeted her, heaving the dog bed on to the counter. "I was wondering if you'd be interested in buying this bed. It's hardly been used at all."

The Pet Finders watched from the other side of the store. "Poor thing. Do you think his dog's died?" Natalie whispered.

"He doesn't look exactly upset if it did," Tristan pointed out. "But I can't see any other reason why anyone would sell a nearly-new dog b—" He broke off suddenly, his eyes gleaming. "Unless he got rid of his dog! By dumping it, maybe?"

"Oh, no, Tris," Andi said. "You can't be suggesting he's the puppy's owner."

"He *could* be," Tristan insisted. He moved closer to the counter, eyeing the man suspiciously.

"It would be too much of a coincidence that we're

in Christine's shop when the puppy's owner turns up, trying to sell her bed," Andi hissed, pulling Tristan behind a stand displaying pet toys. "And don't make it so obvious that we're eavesdropping!" She picked up a rubber bone and began to examine it.

"In any case," Natalie added, "I keep telling you, that puppy wasn't dumped. Her owners are probably searching frantically for her right now."

"Yeah, right," Tristan said. "Let's listen to what he's saying," he added hurriedly, as Natalie opened her mouth to argue.

"It's in perfect condition," the man said. "My puppy only used it for a few weeks. She's growing so quickly, she won't fit into it any more."

"That basket's huge!" Tristan whispered, peering around the pet toy stand. "His dog must be a monster if it can't fit in there."

"I'm afraid I don't sell second-hand equipment," Christine said. "Sorry."

The man shrugged. "Thanks anyway," he said, before picking up the dog basket and going out.

Tristan darted to the counter. "Do you know him, Christine?" he demanded. "Is he one of your regular customers?"

"No, I've never seen him before. Why?"

"Tristan thinks he's the puppy's owner," Andi explained.

Christine frowned. "He said his dog had *outgrown* the basket, not that he'd *lost* his dog."

"Yeah, but nobody has a dog too big for a basket that size," Tristan argued.

"Maybe it's a St Bernard or a Great Dane," Christine said. "They get pretty big."

"Or, maybe he doesn't need a bed any more because he dumped his dog on the main road out of Aldcliffe!" Tristan countered.

"But the bed was too big for a puppy," Andi pointed out. She realized that she was still holding the rubber bone and hung it on the display stand again.

"Lots of people buy beds for their puppies that will be big enough for them when they're fully grown," Christine said. "It's expensive having to buy two beds of different sizes."

"There you are, then!" Tristan exclaimed. He ran to the door and looked along the street.

"Not that I'm agreeing with what Tristan's saying," Christine added. "I'm just giving you the facts."

"The puppy wasn't dumped," Natalie said determinedly. "You're completely wrong about this, Tris. Tell him, Andi!"

But before Andi could say anything, Tristan turned round, his eyes gleaming mischievously. "The man's looking in the baker's window, just down the road!" he whispered. "Let's follow him and see where he goes."

Chapter Six

Andi cringed. Suppose Tristan was right about the man with the dog basket being the puppy's owner? If they didn't follow him, they could miss out on the chance to solve another case. Though, if the puppy *had* been abandoned, she wasn't sure she even wanted to track down her owners.

"Come on!" Tristan urged, beckoning. "He'll get away if we don't hurry."

"OK," Andi agreed. "I guess there's no harm in following him. Come on, Nat."

"But . . ." Natalie protested.

Tristan grabbed her arm and marched her outside. Andi followed them, still not sure that they were doing the right thing.

"There he goes!" Tristan hissed. The man was walking slowly along the pavement, with the basket under his arm.

"Remember the way we suspected all the wrong people when Christine's animals were stolen from Paws for Thought?" Natalie said. "We're making the same mistake again. This man's not the puppy's owner, I'm sure of it."

"But what if he is and we let him go?" Andi countered. "I know Tristan jumps to wild conclusions sometimes—"

"I do not!"

Andi ignored him. "But he might be right one of these days. And what if today's the day? There's no harm in checking this man out."

"He's acting really suspicious," Tristan insisted. "Puppies don't grow as fast as that."

"His story does sound pretty unlikely," Natalie agreed. "I suppose Andi's right. There's no harm in following him."

They set off along the pavement. Soon, the man crossed the road and turned into a side street. The Pet Finders sped up. Halfway down the street, he stopped by a parked car and rummaged in his pockets.

"Uh-oh. He's going to drive away," Tristan groaned.

The man unlocked his car, placed the dog bed on the passenger seat, and climbed in.

The Pet Finders looked at each other in dismay. "Let's get closer," Tristan urged. "At least I'll be able to memorize the number plate." He began to run, and Andi and Natalie raced after him.

"What good will that do?" Natalie puffed. "We can't track him down with a number plate. Only the police can do that."

Tristan didn't answer; he just kept running.

The car pulled away as Tristan reached it. "He's heading this way, Nat," Andi puffed. "Take a picture of him with your mobile phone!"

Natalie pulled it out and flipped it open. As the man drove towards her, she snapped his photo. The car had reached them when suddenly a huge shaggy dog stood up in the back seat. It was so big its head touched the ceiling and its tail brushed the window on the other side.

Andi and Natalie gazed open-mouthed. "He was telling the truth!" Andi gasped. "His dog really *is* enormous."

Tristan came towards them. "Did you see that?" he said in astonishment. "Was that dog massive or was that dog massive? I bet it eats whole cows for breakfast."

"We need a new lead," Andi noted. "Anyone got any ideas?"

"We need to print some posters of the puppy." Natalie glanced at her watch. "But we're too late to take photos of her today. The RSPCA will be closed."

"Tomorrow, then," Andi decided. "We'll take them straight after school."

Andi woke up early the next morning. She opened the curtains, then sat on her windowsill in a patch of sunshine, thinking about the Labrador puppy. Fisher had said that she needed lots of visitors to stop her from getting bored, but the Pet Finders still had to find Shane's missing guinea pig, so they couldn't spend as much time with the puppy as Andi would have liked.

Footsteps sounded on the pavement outside. Twisting round, she saw Mike the postman out for an early-morning jog. Her thoughts switched to the way he had been so nervous about delivering a parcel to the house where he'd heard a big dog barking.

What he needs is a crash course in getting on with dogs, she thought to herself. And suddenly, she knew just the dog to help him! Buddy! He was small and friendly, and very obedient when he was in the right mood. No one could be frightened of him.

70

"Mike!" she called, leaning out of the window.

The postman glanced round, surprised.

"Up here!"

Mike looked up at her.

"Hang on!" Andi called. "I've got an idea!" She dressed hurriedly and rushed downstairs. Buddy came scampering out of the kitchen, his tail wagging furiously. "No early walk this morning, Bud," Andi told him. She gave him a quick pat, then let herself out of the front door.

Mike was waiting on the pavement, looking puzzled. "What idea?" He smiled at Andi.

"To cure your fear of dogs!"

His smile vanished. "It doesn't involve me getting close to one, does it?"

"You wouldn't be frightened if you realized how friendly they are," Andi insisted.

Mike gave a hollow laugh. "They're not friendly to me." He held up his bandaged hand. "They're downright vicious."

"Come and meet Buddy. He'll show you that most dogs aren't like that."

"No, thanks."

"Come on, Buddy's only small," Andi said persuasively. "He wouldn't hurt a fly."

71

Mike pushed back his baseball cap and shrugged. "I suppose I could give it a try."

"Great! Come on." Andi led the way back to her house, then raced up the driveway. Mike followed more slowly.

As Andi opened the front door, Buddy came bursting out. Mike stopped and eyed the little Jack Russell warily as he darted towards him.

"Here, Bud!" Andi called.

Buddy trotted back to her at once, his stumpy tail wagging. Andi grinned with relief. Buddy was obviously in the right mood.

"I'll put him on his lead," she told Mike, clipping it to his collar. "There. Now, come a bit closer."

Mike approached slowly.

"Sit, Buddy!" Andi commanded. Buddy sat down. "See how good he is?" Andi said.

Mike reached the steps leading up to the front porch. "He knows I'm afraid of him," he fretted.

"Don't worry, dogs forgive anything." *Even being abandoned?* Andi wondered silently, picturing the Labrador pup's adorable little face.

"So what do you want me to do now?" Mike asked.

"Come and stroke him."

73

Mike leapt back. "Not likely!"

"He won't hurt you, I promise."

Mike swallowed hard. He took a step towards Buddy, then stopped again. "He's got sharp teeth."

"Buddy has *never* bitten anyone. And he's not going to start now." Andi was sure she was on the right track. Once Mike had stroked Buddy, he'd be well on the way to conquering his fear of dogs. "Go on, stroke his head."

Mike took another step forward, then reached towards him. Buddy sat still, his tail wagging.

Mike gently touched the top of Buddy's head with one finger. Buddy's tail wagged harder. "See?" Andi said. "He likes you."

Mike tickled his ears, but Andi could see from the strained expression on his face that he expected Buddy to bite him at any moment.

Suddenly, a cat appeared at the end of the driveway. Buddy sprang up with a loud bark and Mike leapt back. He landed awkwardly on the bottom step and fell over backwards.

Buddy jerked on his lead. It slipped through Andi's fingers and he went tearing across the front lawn. The cat took off, scrambling over a fence with a rattle of claws. Buddy raced after it, barking furiously. 'Buddy!" Andi yelled. "Come here!"

Buddy skidded to a halt, and then he slunk slowly back to the house with his tail between his legs and his lead trailing behind him.

"I'm really sorry, Mike," Andi said, helping him up. "Are you all right?"

"I think so," he said, nodding. "Listen, it was good of you to try to help me. Maybe I'd get over my fear of dogs if I knew some friendly ones, but I think Buddy's a bit too lively for me."

Andi shrugged. "You're probably right. But it might be worth trying again."

"No, thanks. What I need is a small, *quiet* dog to start me off. Anyway, I'd better get going." He jogged away down the street.

Andi went indoors, thinking about what Mike had said. "I know an ideal small, quiet dog," she told Buddy. "The dog with no name! She'd be perfect." She hurriedly unclipped Buddy's lead. "Stay, Bud," she said, then she dashed back outside.

She caught up with Mike at the end of the street. "Hey, I know the perfect dog!" she called. "She's a little Labrador puppy. She's not very well at the moment, because she was hit by a car, but she's really friendly. You'll love her, Mike, I just know it!"

"I don't know . . ."

"Come and meet her," Andi pleaded.

He smiled. "Maybe. If she really *is* quiet."

"Definitely. Can you meet me at four o'clock outside the RSPCA centre?"

"I'll be there," Mike promised. "I can tell I won't get any peace until I say yes."

Straight after breakfast, Andi grabbed her mum's digital camera. She planned to take a few photos of the Labrador puppy while she was at the RSPCA with Mike. Then the Pet Finders could start working on the posters.

As she put the camera into her rucksack, her mum came out into the hall. "What are you doing, Andi?"

Andi explained about the photos.

Her mum shook her head. "I'm sorry, darling, but that camera's too valuable to take to school. You could lose it."

"But, Mum!"

"No," Mrs Talbot said firmly. "You're not taking it, Andi, and that's final."

"Could you meet me after school then, and bring the camera with you? It's really important. I won't have time to come home and get it. I'm meeting Mike

Morgan at the RSPCA straight after school."

Her mum sighed. "I can't today. I've got meetings all afternoon, darling."

"Mum!" Andi groaned.

This was the Pet Finders' hardest case yet. No one seemed to have lost a dog, and now they couldn't even make posters!

Chapter Seven

Mike was waiting for the Pet Finders when they arrived at the RSPCA centre after school. "Hello there! I bet you thought I wouldn't turn up."

"Of course not," Andi said, but she was secretly relieved to see him. After the way Buddy had behaved that morning, she'd been afraid he might have turned Mike off dogs for life.

Fisher was sitting in the reception area, doing some paperwork, when they went into the centre. "Hello," he said. "Come to see the puppy?"

"This is Mike Morgan, our postman," Andi explained. "He wants to meet her."

"How is she today?" Natalie asked.

"Much better," Fisher said. "How are you doing with tracking down her owners? Molly's been phoning some other RSPCA centres to see if anyone's reported losing a Labrador, but we haven't heard of anyone yet."

"We're still working on it," Tristan said.

"We were going to take some photos of her today," Andi told him, "but I wasn't allowed to take our camera to school, so we'll have to fit it in another time."

They went through to see the dog with no name. She was lying in her bed, but she stood up as soon as she saw them. "She doesn't look so stiff today," Andi said, feeling pleased.

"And her cuts seem to be healing," Tristan added.

"What do you think, Mike?" Natalie asked. "Do you like the look of her?"

"She looks pretty safe, so far," Mike said. "It's a shame all dogs aren't as small and cute as this one."

"She won't be this small for ever," Andi warned him.

"Now she tells me!" He heaved a melodramatic sigh.

They opened the cage, and the puppy trotted out with her tail wagging and her clean golden fur shining.

"She is so gorgeous!" Natalie exclaimed. She reached into the cage to pick up a ball and rolled it across the floor. The puppy trotted after it. She carried the ball back and dropped it at Natalie's feet. As she reached for it, Andi grabbed her arm.

"Let Mike play with her," she whispered.

"Huh? Oh, all right." Natalie looked puzzled, but she handed the ball to Mike. He rolled it away and the puppy trotted off to fetch it, wagging her tail harder than ever. When she brought it back, she pounced on one of Mike's shoelaces and tugged it. 'Hey, she's really playful," he laughed, smiling down at her.

"Will you be all right if we go now, Mike?" Andi asked. "We've got to search for a lost guinea pig."

Natalie and Tristan stared at her in surprise.

"Of course." Mike didn't even glance around; he was too wrapped up in ruffling the pup's ears.

"See you later, then," Andi said. The Pet Finders said goodbye to Fisher and went out into the bright sunshine.

"What was all that about?" Tristan demanded as soon as they were outside. "You got us out of there too fast to not have something up your sleeve."

"It's part of my plan to beat Mike's fear of dogs," Andi explained. "I tried getting him to stroke Buddy this morning, but Bud was too lively."

"And you thought the puppy would be quieter," Natalie said. "Good idea. I hope it works."

"I've been thinking about Cocoa," Tristan said as they headed for Cooper's Hill.

"Careful, Tris," Natalie warned. "You don't want to strain yourself."

Tristan made his usual face at her. "If she *has* been stolen," he went on, "then I think a kid must have taken her, because guinea pigs aren't valuable. It's not as though an adult would steal her to sell. So if a kid took her, we might find her in one of the gardens near the Jupps' house. A kid wouldn't have a car to take her away in."

"That's true," Andi said. "We should look out for hutches while we're searching and try to see what's inside."

They passed a corner shop. "Look!" Natalie exclaimed, stopping beside some postcards that were stuck in the window. One of them had a picture of a golden Labrador puppy on it. FOR SALE, the card said. GOLDEN LABRADOR PUPPIES. There was a phone number at the bottom of the card.

Natalie pulled out her mobile. "Let's give them a ring."

"Why?" Andi asked, puzzled.

"They might have sold the dog with no name." She punched in the number.

After a few moments, she grinned at Tristan and Andi, and gave them a thumbs-up. "Hello?" she said into the phone. "Yes, I saw your postcard advertising puppies for sale. I don't want to buy one, but I'm trying to find the owner of a golden Labrador puppy who's about twelve weeks old. She's had an accident and—"

She broke off and listened for a moment. "Oh, I see." She sounded disappointed. "Do you know any other Labrador breeders who might . . .?" Again she stopped to listen. "Right. OK, thanks." She snapped her phone shut. "No good. The breeder's puppies are only four weeks old and her last litter was born six months ago."

"What about other breeders?" Andi prompted.

Natalie shook her head gloomily. "That woman I spoke to has only just moved to Aldcliffe from Exeter and she doesn't know anyone here yet."

Andi could see her disappointment reflected in Tristan's and Natalie's faces. But they couldn't waste time moping: they had a guinea pig to find.

"Come on," Andi said. "Let's go and look for Cocoa."

They were soon at the Jupps' house. When Tristan rang the bell, Mrs Jupp opened the door. "Have you found her?" she said eagerly.

Shane came running, his face bright with hope. Andi felt really bad about telling him that Cocoa was still missing. "Not yet," she admitted. "We actually came to see if she'd turned up, but I can see she hasn't."

Shane's face fell.

"We saw the posters," Mrs Jupp said, trying to sound positive. "They look lovely. Has anyone rung you yet?"

"No," Andi told her, wishing she had something hopeful to tell the Jupps. "We're going to search around here. Where have you looked so far?"

"In our back garden, and Shane went along the alley behind the house. We've put out a dish of sunflower seeds in case she finds her way back into the garden and gets hungry. They're Cocoa's favourite, but they haven't been touched."

"OK," Andi said. "We'll start looking in the alley." They'd searched the middle part of the alley before, but not the area immediately behind the house or farther up the hill.

"Come through the house," Mrs Jupp offered, opening the door wide.

The Pet Finders made their way through to the garden, and past the dish of sunflower seeds and the hutch where Sugar sat all alone. Shane trailed after them. "I really, really miss Cocoa. You will find her, won't you?"

"We'll do our best," Natalie promised. "Hey, can we

take the dish of sunflower seeds with us? Perhaps she'll hear it rattling and come running."

"OK!" Shane darted off to get it.

They headed uphill first, shaking the sunflower seeds and listening hard for a guinea pig's distinctive *whoop whoop* in reply. But there was nothing to hear except birds singing and a few distant cars. They searched in the long grass and checked around the roots of trees, looking for hollows where a guinea pig might try to keep herself safe.

"Don't forget to look for hutches, too," Tristan reminded them. "She might have been taken to someone else's garden."

Andi stood on tiptoe to look over a fence. 'Nothing in here." She moved to the next garden and peered over the wall. "There's one in this garden. I can barely see the roof. Give me a leg up so I can see inside."

Tristan and Natalie lifted her up.

"I can see a little patch of brown fur! Maybe it's her." Andi craned her neck, her heart thudding with excitement.

"Hurry up!" Natalie grunted. "You're heavy."

Andi leant further over the wall until she could see the creature in the hutch. "It's a rabbit." She dropped down, nearly landing on Tristan's toe.

They set off again.

"There's another hutch here!" Natalie called after a few minutes.

Tristan and Andi ran to see. This hutch stood at the end of a garden that was fenced by a hedge so sparse they could easily see through it. "There's something in there," Natalie said. "I saw it move." She bent a branch aside and pushed through the hedge to look inside the hutch. "It's brown," she said excitedly. Then she drew back, sighing. "I'm not sure what it is, but it's definitely not a guinea pig. It's got a long tail."

Andi and Tristan pulled branches aside so they could look, too. "It's a ferret," Tristan said, disappointed.

Andi glanced back along the alley. They'd come quite a way from the Jupps' back gate. She wasn't sure that Cocoa would have come this far on her own. Guinea pigs had tiny legs, and got tired easily. "I think we should go back and search in the opposite direction," she suggested. "That way—" She broke off as a distinctive squeak rang out.

Chapter Eight

The Pet Finders raced along the alley, following the tiny squeal. The stones beneath their feet slid away as they ran, but they couldn't slow down: if the squeaking stopped, they might not be able to find the garden the noise had come from.

Despite the uneven ground, Andi was soon quite a way ahead of Tristan and Natalie. The squeak was much louder now; she could hear it clearly above the crunch of the stones under her feet. She stopped running and looked round. The sound was coming from behind a high wood-panelled fence.

Andi ran to the fence and sprang into the air, but she couldn't see over it. There was no way she could climb the fence: the boards were perfectly smooth. "I can't see over," she said, as Natalie and Tristan came panting up.

"Let me get my breath back, then we'll try lifting you," Tristan puffed.

Natalie bent over, hands on knees, breathing hard. She didn't look as if she could hoist a blade of grass into the air at that point.

Andi looked round. There was a tall tree growing outside the neighbouring garden. "It's OK, I can climb that tree," she said.

She swung herself on to the lowest branch. She still couldn't see over the fence, so she climbed on to the next branch, and then the next. At last, she could see right into the garden. A guinea pig's hutch was standing against the fence on one side. And to Andi's horror, a fat tabby cat was hunched in front of the hutch, gazing in through the wire. No wonder the guinea pig was making so much noise!

"Shoo!" Andi yelled.

Her shout startled the cat. It spun round, but then leapt on to the roof of the hutch, its claws scratching against the waterproof felt.

"What is it?" Tristan looked up at Andi, his freckled face anxious.

"There's a cat hanging around the hutch."

The cat stretched one paw over the edge of the roof, hooked its claws through the wire, and began to pull. The frightened guinea pig raced up and down, squeaking at the top of its voice. Andi could see that it wasn't Cocoa; it had smooth ginger-and-white fur instead.

"Get away!" she shouted at the cat.

It looked up at her, then yanked at the wire again. To Andi's relief, the door stayed shut. But, all the same, she had to help the panic-stricken guinea pig. *Not just Pet Finders — Pet Rescuers, as well*, she thought. She stretched up and caught hold of one of the branches near the top of the tree, then shook it as hard as she could, making the leaves swish and rustle.

The noise wasn't loud, but it was enough to frighten the cat. It leapt off the hutch on to the fence and scrambled to the top, its claws scratching madly. It teetered at the top for a moment, looking from Andi to the hutch, and back again; then it vanished into the next garden.

Andi climbed down from the tree. "It's gone," she puffed, wiping her hands on her jeans.

"Was it Cocoa?" Natalie asked.

"No. But the hutch was the same as Cocoa's and the cat couldn't get the door open." She paused. "I don't see how Cocoa could have got out by herself. If a cat couldn't open the door, there's no chance of a guinea pig doing it."

"She *must* have been stolen then," Tristan said.

"Let's not tell Shane right away," Andi said, imagining his dismay. "Perhaps the posters will do some good. Someone might see Cocoa in a neighbour's back garden and phone us." At this point, Andi almost hoped the guinea pig *had* been stolen. At least then, Cocoa would be shut up in a hutch and safe. If she was out on her own with a hungry cat on the prowl . . . Andi shuddered.

"We haven't finished searching yet," Natalie reminded them.

They went on along the alley, but there was no sign of Cocoa anywhere. There were no more hutches, either. At last, they reached the part of the alley that they'd already searched. "She's not here," Tristan said glumly.

Andi glanced at her watch. "There's still time to get my camera and take a few photos of the puppy before the RSPCA closes for the night." It would be good to have something positive to do.

"Will it involve running?" Natalie asked. "I've had more than enough exercise for one day, thank you."

Andi laughed. "No. We've got enough time to walk. Come on."

Buddy was sitting in the hall when the Pet Finders reached Andi's house. He sprang up at them, barking excitedly.

"What's up, Bud?" Andi said. She crouched down to stroke him, and he leapt on to her lap and licked her cheek. Then he jumped down again and went racing round Tristan and Natalie.

Andi's mum came into the hall. "Thank goodness you're home, Andi," she said, raising her voice to make herself heard above Buddy's excited barks. "Buddy's had a crazy half hour. He's been racing up and down the stairs and barking every time a car goes by. Could you take him for a walk, please?" She disappeared into the kitchen again, clearly agitated by Buddy's behaviour.

"OK," Andi called after her. 'We're going to see the puppy. It'll be good for her to meet another dog!" She fetched her mum's camera, then went into the kitchen. "Can I take a corncob? Remember how much Buddy liked them when he was young? I thought the puppy might like them, too."

"Help yourself. There's a pack in the fridge," her mum replied.

Andi took a cob and went back into the hall. Tristan was holding Buddy in his arms and the little dog was licking his nose. "Pets are so great," he laughed. "But even *you're* not as great as Lucy, Bud."

Andi clipped on Buddy's lead. "It must be the spring weather making him behave like this," she said. "Perhaps he remembers all the sunshine we used to have when we lived in Texas." She could hardly believe that she'd been living in Aldcliffe for nine whole months. She lifted Buddy out of Tristan's arms and set him down on the floor.

"Phew!" Tristan joked. "He almost washed my whole nose right off."

The little Jack Russell dashed to the door and pressed his nose to the crack, impatient to be let out. "See you later, Mum!" Andi called as Buddy yanked her out of the front door and down the driveway.

The dog with no name was chewing the edge of her basket when they got to the RSPCA centre.

"Hello, girl," Natalie said, opening the cage door.

The puppy ran out, her tail wagging, and her soft thick ears pricked, then darted away down the room.

"Did you see that?" Tristan asked. "She actually *ran*. She must be feeling better. Fisher was right about that dislocated hip. You'd never know she had an injured leg a couple of days ago."

"And her cuts hardly show at all," Natalie added. "She'll look great in the pictures."

The puppy trotted back to them, her brown eyes shining. She and Buddy touched noses, then the little Labrador darted away to fetch her ball. She retrieved it and dropped it by Buddy's front paws.

"She's really good at fetching things," Tristan said.

"That's what Labradors do," Andi told him. "Their real name is Labrador retriever. People who go out shooting often have them as pets, to bring back pheasants or whatever."

Buddy looked up at Andi and barked. "OK, boy!" she said. "You can play for a while, but don't go wearing the puppy out."

As soon as he was off his lead, Buddy grabbed the ball and went tearing round the room with it wedged in his mouth. The puppy scampered after him, yapping with excitement.

"We have *got* to think of a name for her," Natalie said. She clutched Andi's arm. "Hang on! I've got the perfect name for her! Amabel."

"Amabel?" Tristan hooted.

"It's my cousin's name. It means lovable."

"Good grief," he said, rolling his eyes to the ceiling. "The puppy *is* lovable. It really suits her."

"It's a horrible name," Tristan said.

"You like it, don't you, Andi?" Natalie said hopefully.

Andi made a face. "Not really. I mean, it's OK for a person, but it just doesn't sound like a dog's name."

The door of Fisher's office opened. "I should have known you three would be behind this mayhem," he joked. He watched as the dog with no name lay down right in front of Buddy, forcing him to jump over her, his stumpy legs at full stretch. "I think she was still feeling the after-effects of the anaesthetic when you were here earlier, but it's obviously worn off now. Her bruises are nearly gone, too, and the cuts are healing nicely. Any luck with finding her owner?"

"Not yet, so we've come to take some pictures of her for the posters," Andi said, holding up her camera.

"Good luck! Let's hope you can keep her still long enough to take them. Oh, and by the way, Mike was terrific with her. Very gentle. I hope he can find time to come again." Fisher went back into his office again.

"Hey, look at Buddy," Natalie said.

He had gone into the cage and was lying in the

puppy's basket, panting hard. The puppy was trying to make him play again, picking up the ball and dropping it beside him over and over.

Andi laughed. "I've never seen Buddy worn out from playing before!"

"He did run about twenty miles on the way here," Natalie reminded her. They'd cut across the park and Buddy had raced in giant circles the moment he was let off his lead. "He must have run round the pond a hundred times."

"Well I hope he's not too exhausted to walk home," Andi said. "I don't fancy the idea of carrying him all the way. He may be small, but he's pretty heavy."

"I'll play with you, girl," Tristan told the puppy. He threw the ball across the room, then sat down and waited for the pup to bring it back to him. She bounded after it, her ears flopping and her huge paws almost tripping her up. Snatching it, she galloped back and dropped the ball beside Tristan. As he reached for it, the puppy darted behind him and snatched the red notebook out of his pocket.

"Hey, give that back!" Tristan scolded.

The puppy looked up at him with her head on one side, then scurried to the other end of the room with the notebook in her mouth. Tristan jumped up to run after her, but she dodged him and squeezed behind a chair.

"Come on, you two! Give me a hand here," Tristan puffed.

Andi and Natalie were laughing too hard to reply.

The Labrador lay down in the corner and began to chew the notebook. "Help me get it back!" Tristan begged. "It's got all our case notes in it."

Still laughing, Andi took the corncob out of her rucksack and held it out to the puppy. With that, she quickly abandoned the notebook and took the corn, then lay down to gnaw it, her tail thumping against the ground.

"Take her picture!" Natalie urged. "Before she starts tearing around again."

Andi snapped a few shots while Tristan grabbed his notebook. As was expected, the cover was dotted with tiny teeth marks. "Typical!" he joked. "You try and help lost puppies and all they do is eat your stuff!"

When Andi was satisfied with the photos, she clipped Buddy's lead back on. "Let's go, boy. Time to get home."

The little Labrador trotted over, holding the corn in her mouth. The two dogs sniffed each other briefly, then the puppy climbed into her basket, flopped

down, and began to gnaw the corn again.

"Bye, girl," Andi said. She patted the pup's soft golden head before fastening the cage door. "She seems pretty happy here," she remarked as she straightened up.

"That's because she's so sweet-natured," Natalie pointed out. "But we really have got to step up the search for her owner. I can't think of a dog that deserves a better home than she does!"

"Let's write 'the Dog with No Name' at the top of the posters," Natalie suggested, when they were sitting down in Andi's mum's study later.

"Great idea!" Andi agreed. "People will be really intrigued." She typed it in, then pasted in her favourite photo of the selection they'd taken earlier. It showed the puppy looking straight into the lens, her soft ears pricked up as though she were listening.

"What else do we need to write?"

"How about 'Do you know this puppy?'" said Tristan, crouching down to tickle Buddy.

The little Jack Russell rolled over so Tristan could rub his tummy, then squirmed over again, sprang up, and licked Tristan's cheek. "Yuck! Get off, Bud. I'm clean enough, thanks."

"That's what you think," Natalie said. "But Buddy knows better."

"There!" Andi clicked on the print button. "We're definitely getting faster at making posters." As the first one came spooling out of the printer, she picked it up. "We'll put these up after dinner, OK?" She sighed. "Let's hope they work. We haven't had much luck with the puppy or with Cocoa so far."

"I know what you mean," Natalie agreed. "I really hope we're not going to fail with these two cases."

They looked at each other gloomily, until Buddy sprang into the middle of the room and began to chase his tail. Then they all laughed.

"Thanks, Bud. You know how to cheer people up, don't you?" Tristan said.

Andi glanced at the poster again. "We can't keep calling her 'the dog with no name'." She stared hard at the photo, trying to come up with an idea. "Hey! How about Beauty? She's so pretty it fits her perfectly."

Tristan snorted. "Beauty? I don't think so."

"Why not? She's lovely."

"It's not right for her," Natalie said. "She's pretty all right, but she's too energetic. A dog called Beauty should walk around elegantly, not charge up and down like a mad thing."

Tristan waved his notebook under Andi's nose. 'Dogs called Beauty don't go around wrecking people's notebooks."

"OK," Andi said, "but we've got to call her something."

"Dinner's ready!" Mrs Talbot called up the stairs.

Tristan leapt up. "Fantastic, I'm starving!" He raced out of the study and down the stairs.

"Do you know who he reminds me of?" Natalie sighed.

"Who?" Andi asked.

"My dog," she replied.'"Jet comes running too, when I call him for his dinner."

Chapter Nine

After school the next day, the Pet Finders headed for the Banana Beach Café. It was the sunniest place in Aldcliffe, with yellow walls and rainbow-coloured umbrellas shading the tables outside. Today, with the sun shining so brightly, the café looked dazzling.

"Whoa, I should have brought my shades," Tristan said, as they stood opposite the café, waiting to cross the road.

"The puppy posters look good," Natalie noted, pointing to one on a nearby lamppost. They'd put nearly all of them up the evening before. "I wonder if anyone phoned while we were at school."

"I'll check," Andi said. She took out her mobile phone and rang her mum.

"Sorry, darling. No messages," Mrs Talbot answered.

Andi hung up and shook her head. 'No."

Suddenly her phone began to ring. Her heart jumped and she answered quickly. "Hello?"

"Hi," said a man's voice. "Is this Andi?"

"Yes."

"This is Tim Saunders, Tristan's dad. Sorry to bother you, but he hardly ever carries his mobile phone and I need to speak to him."

"Don't worry, he's right here, Mr Saunders."

Tristan's eyebrows shot up as she passed the phone to him. "Hello, Dad. What's up?" There was a pause while he listened, then his face lit up. "Fantastic! Thanks, Dad."

"Share the good news," Natalie prompted when he ended the call.

"I've been hoping this would work out all day," Tristan said, beaming at her and Andi. "But I didn't want to mention it before, just in case it didn't."

"What?" Natalie said impatiently. "Don't keep us waiting."

Tristan spread his hands wide like a magician. "The puppy's going to be in the local paper tomorrow! My dad knows the editor and she sent a photographer to the RSPCA today to take the puppy's picture. They've written an article asking if anyone knows who she belongs to."

"You are amazing, Tris!" Andi whooped.

But Natalie nudged her. "Watch it! Don't give him an excuse for an even bigger ego!" Then she laughed. "Seriously, it's great news, Tris. I bet someone will claim the puppy as soon as the paper comes out."

They crossed the road to the café. Jango and Maggie Pearce – Fisher's parents, and owners of the café – were sitting outside, poring over a street map of Aldcliffe.

"Hi, Maggie. Hi, Jango," Tristan called.

"Tristan! And Andi and Natalie!" Maggie jumped up. She was a round-faced Jamaican woman with a broad welcoming smile. As always, she was wearing a bright sunshine-yellow dress. "How you doin'? You still searching for lost pets?"

"Yep," Andi said. She glanced at the map. "Are you trying to find somewhere? Tristan can probably tell you how to get there. He knows just about every road in Aldcliffe."

"Mansfield Road," Jango said. He was a middle-aged man with grey hair growing in tufts on either side of his head. "There's a new flour mill there and we heard their flour's the best anywhere. We only want the best for our banana muffins! But the writing on this map is so small we can hardly make it out."

"It's on the east side of town," Tristan told him. "Almost out in the country. Look." He bent over the map. "Here."

"Tristan, you are a wonder, boy," Jango said, slapping him on the back. "It's lucky you three are such regular customers. We could have been searching for hours if you hadn't turned up. Now, what can we get you?"

"Banana flapjacks and apple juice, please," Tristan said.

"You sitting outside in the sunshine?" Maggie asked.

"Yes, please," Natalie replied. "It's too nice to be indoors on a day like this."

"Be right out," Maggie said, and disappeared inside with Jango.

Andi was still looking at the map. "Isn't this where we found the puppy?" She ran her finger along the main road that headed south from Aldcliffe.

"That's right," Tristan said.

"I wonder where her owners were going?" Natalie said, sounding puzzled. "That road looks as though it goes straight out of town."

Andi's stomach turned over. She'd been trying not to believe Tristan's theory that the puppy had been dumped, but too many things seemed to point to it. For a start, nobody had reported the dog missing. Nobody had phoned since the posters went up, either, though the town centre was filled with them, and it would be hard for anyone to miss them. Finally, and most importantly, the puppy had been found on a busy road that headed straight out of town.

"Maybe they *were* heading out of town," Andi said. "Maybe they were leaving Aldcliffe for good." She shivered. "You might be right after all, Tris – about her being dumped."

Natalie started to argue, but Tristan interrupted. 'Let's think about this logically. If Andi's right and her owners have moved out of town, then that would give them the perfect opportunity to dump her."

"Their old neighbours wouldn't know the puppy had disappeared," Andi said angrily, "and their new ones wouldn't know they'd ever owned a dog."

Natalie shook her head. "I don't believe it. She's too lovable just to be thrown away."

Just then, Mike Morgan came jogging along the road. He spotted the Pet Finders and came over to speak to them. "Hey, am I glad to see you!" He dropped into the empty chair at their table. 'Marathon-training can get a bit lonely."

"Do you run marathons at this time of year?" Tristan asked.

"Training for them is a year-round job." Mike's eyes twinkled. "And you never know, I might find a publisher for my book, and I'll have to look good for the publicity photos." He had told Andi he was writing a book called *Mad Mike Morgan's Marathon Manual*. "Anyway," he continued, "I want to hear how the puppy's doing. I've seen posters of her all over town. Have you found her owners yet?"

"Not yet," Andi admitted. "We were wondering if they might have moved out of town . . ." She trailed off and stared at Mike. "You're a postman. You must know who's moved away recently."

"Yes, I know a few families."

"Can you give us their names, so we can find out whether any of them used to have a golden Lab?"

Mike thought for a moment. "Hmm."

Tristan handed Mike the red notebook. "You can write them in here."

Mike fingered the tooth-marked cover and

grinned. "Looks like you three have been having a bit of dog trouble, too."

Maggie came out of the café carrying a tray of apple juice and flapjacks while Mike was writing the list. There was a yellow paper umbrella and a rainbow-coloured straw in every glass. "Hello there, Mike," she said. "Can I get you something? A banana sandwich, maybe, to keep your strength up?"

"No, thanks, Mrs P. I'll be off in a minute." He wrote down the last name. "Those are the only ones I can think of off the top of my head. If I remember any others, I'll put the names through your letterbox with your post tomorrow, Andi." He stood up. "I might see you when I visit the puppy."

"He seems to be getting on really well with the dog with no name," Andi said as he jogged away.

They read through Mike's list of names as they sipped their apple juice. There were twelve altogether. "It'll take ages to check all these," Natalie sighed. "I wonder if we can trim it down?"

Tristan stabbed his finger down on a name. "These people, the Wilkinsons, haven't got a dog. James Wilkinson's a friend of Dean's and I went to his flat a few times." He crossed them off, then sat staring into space.

"What are you thinking about?" Andi asked.

"That we should find out which of these other people lived in flats, too. People in flats wouldn't own dogs."

Andi shook her head. "People in flats would be more likely to abandon a puppy. Perhaps they thought it would be nice to have a dog, but once they got one, they found they needed a garden and more space."

"So, what are we going to do?" Tristan broke off a piece of flapjack and put it in his mouth.

"Christine might recognize some of these names," Andi said. "She could eliminate people with cats who might not have a dog, or true dog-lovers who'd never dump a pet in a million years."

"I'll ask her tomorrow. I'm helping out at the shop in the morning."

"Hang on. Shouldn't we tell Shane that we think Cocoa's been stolen?" Andi pointed out. Then she made a face. "Though, I'm not looking forward to it much."

"We should all go together tomorrow," Tristan said. "I'll be finished by eleven. Can you wait until then?"

"OK. Are you free then, Nat?"

"Yeah. Do you want to take Buddy and Jet for a

walk before that? We could go and visit the puppy, too."

"Great idea," Andi agreed.

Tristan ate the last morsel of his flapjack and drained his glass. He looked hopefully at Andi's flapjack. She'd been so busy thinking about the list of names that she hadn't eaten it yet. "I don't suppose you've finished with that, have you?" he asked hopefully.

"No, she hasn't," Natalie answered on Andi's behalf. She wrapped the flapjack in a paper napkin. "She was planning to eat it on the way home," she said, and pushed it into Andi's pocket.

Andi laughed. "Sorry, Tris, but there's no way I'd miss out on Jango's cooking. His flapjacks are to die for."

Tristan sighed, then put the notebook into his rucksack. "Then I'm not sure I'll be able to ask Christine about this tomorrow," he said in a faint voice.

"Why not?" Andi asked anxiously. "It was your idea."

"Because I might die of hunger on my way home."

Natalie patted his arm. "Don't worry, Andi and I will come to your funeral." She linked arms with Andi and they set off down the road together.

"Hey, wait for me!" Tristan ran after them.

"Look at that," Natalie laughed. "A miracle recovery! Now let's hope we get another miracle to help us solve these cases."

Chapter Ten

Andi and Buddy arrived at the RSPCA centre at ten o'clock the next morning. It was another beautiful day and Buddy was full of energy.

"Calm down, Bud," Andi said, as they waited outside for Natalie and Jet.

Buddy jumped up and planted his front paws on her leg. His mouth was open in a wide grin.

Natalie and Jet appeared at the end of the road. Jet spotted Buddy and gave a friendly bark. Buddy began to pull towards him, his tail wagging eagerly.

"Hi," Natalie said. "Sorry I'm late. I couldn't decide what to wear."

"I'm not surprised. Nice top, by the way." Natalie was wearing a lilac T-shirt with a sequin star on one shoulder.

"Thanks," Natalie replied. "I got it for my birthday,

but I've only worn it a couple of times. Are those combats new?"

"Yep." Andi did a twirl to show them off.

Molly was feeding the baby bird again when they went into the clinic. "Hi," she said. "Come to see the puppy?"

"Yeah," Andi said. "And then we're taking Buddy and Jet for a walk in the park."

Molly suddenly looked hopeful. "I don't suppose you could take the puppy, too, could you? She's fit enough for more exercise now, and Fisher's given her the injections she needs." The baby bird began to chirp loudly and Molly dropped a morsel of meat into its beak with a pair of tweezers.

"Of course!" Andi exclaimed.

The puppy was very excited to be outdoors. Her paws seemed to go everywhere but in a straight line while she trotted beside Buddy and Jet. Her head turned constantly from side to side as she tried to look in every direction at once. She was the most inquisitive creature Andi had ever seen! A fly buzzed past and she snapped at it, then stopped dead to sniff a flower. The pollen made her sneeze and she shook her head, her brown eyes wide with astonishment.

"You remember when we found Apple?" Natalie asked slowly.

"Yeah?"

Natalie frowned. "Look, I know it's a long shot, but she was excited about lorries because her owner was a lorry driver. Perhaps the dog with no name will get excited about a particular colour or make of car, and that might help us find her owners."

"It's worth a try. Let's take her up to the main road where we found her."

The road was packed with traffic when they arrived. As soon as they started walking along the pavement beside the ditch, the puppy began to tremble. She yapped bravely at a few racing cars, then tucked her tail between her legs and scuttled behind Andi, where she pressed herself against Andi's legs.

"I don't think this is going to work," Andi said. "She looks petrified." She picked the puppy up, trying to comfort her.

The little Labrador buried her face in Andi's shoulder. She was shaking all over. Buddy and Jet watched curiously with their heads on one side.

"Let's go," Andi muttered, swallowing a lump in her throat. "This isn't fair to her."

They hurried back, leaving the roaring traffic behind them.

When they were halfway down a quiet road, the puppy opened one eye and looked round.

"It's all right, girl. The cars are gone," Andi told her.

The puppy sat up in her arms and checked in every direction, then nudged Andi's chin with her head as if to tell her that she wanted to walk. Andi set her down and she trotted between Buddy and Jet, her tail wagging again.

"Poor little thing," Andi sighed. "It's no wonder she's terrified of traffic. She was hit by a car, after all."

"And perhaps she associates cars with her owner," Natalie added grimly. "If she *was* dumped from a car, it's pretty likely that she'd be scared. It was a stupid idea. I should have realized how frightened she'd be."

Andi stared at her. "So you think she was dumped, too?"

Natalie nodded sadly. "I really hate the idea, but . . ." She shrugged. "Why hasn't anyone come forward to claim her? We've put up enough posters and she's even been in the paper."

Andi watched as the puppy leapt up at Jet and nipped his ear. It made her heart ache to think that anyone could abandon such an adorable creature.

They kept to quiet roads as they made their way to the Jupps' house. Tristan was sitting on a garden wall, waiting for them, when they arrived. He waved a piece of paper at them as they approached. "I've been through the list of names with Christine." He spread it out on the wall, then snatched it up hastily as the puppy tried to bite the corner. "No you don't, girl," he laughed, stroking her head.

"Did Christine recognize any of them?" Natalie asked.

"Four out of twelve. She seems to know just about every pet-lover in Aldcliffe – and where they all live. None of the four had yellow Labs before they moved away."

"So, if you take off the Wilkinsons, we've still got to investigate seven people," Natalie said. "That's going to take a bit of time."

"Nope." Tristan said. "You're forgetting that my mum and dad have an estate agency. They knew some of the names, too. Four more, to be exact."

"So, we've only got three names left on the list?"

"Yep."

"That's fantastic, Tris!" Andi exclaimed. "And—"

"Come on," Natalie interrupted. "We've got to break the news to Shane." She started up the driveway.

"I think we should get Shane's mum to call the police," Andi said quietly.

"But they're hardly likely to send out a squad car for a missing guinea pig," Natalie pointed out.

"Perhaps other people have lost pets from their gardens, too."

"Yeah, could be." Natalie shrugged as she stepped on to the Jupps' porch. She seemed really down, even though it wasn't really her fault the puppy had got upset on the busy main road. "But we probably would have heard about them. We are the Pet Finders, don't forget."

Shane flung the front door open before they reached it. "Have you found her?" Mrs Jupp appeared behind him, looking anxious.

"I'm afraid not," Andi confessed.

Shane's bottom lip began to tremble and tears welled up in his eyes.

"Let's go into your back garden," Andi said hurriedly. "So we can tell you what we think."

Mrs Jupp took Shane's hand and the Pet Finders followed them along the side of the house, exchanging worried glances. They'd never had to tell a pet owner that they were giving up a search before.

"The thing is, Shane," Andi began when they were

in the back garden, "we've looked all along the alley and in your neighbours' gardens and there's just no sign of Cocoa anywhere." She went to the hutch. "This bolt is very strong and we don't think Cocoa could have escaped by herself."

Shane stared at her wide-eyed, waiting for her to go on, but the words felt as though they were jammed in her throat.

"We think she must have been stolen," Natalie finished for her.

Mrs Jupp gasped and Shane burst into tears. His mum tried to hug him, but he pushed her away. "Will the police come?" he sobbed.

"Not for a—" Natalie began, but Tristan kicked her.

"It'd be kind of cool if they did," he said, and Andi guessed he was trying to cheer Shane up. After all, kids loved police cars, didn't they? "Especially if their car has the siren going and lights flashing!"

Shane cried harder than ever.

"Come here, darling," Mrs Jupp said. She moved towards him but he darted away again.

"Nice one, Tris," Natalie hissed.

"I d-don't want the police to come!" Shane wailed.

"Why not?" Andi asked. "They might find Cocoa and bring her home."

"Because I t-told a lie and I'll g-get into trouble."

The Pet Finders stared at him.

"What lie?" asked Mrs Jupp, perplexed.

"C-Cocoa wasn't in her hutch. I left her out in the garden by accident when . . . when you told me to clean my room. I f-forgot she was out and . . . and then we w-went sh-shopping . . ."

"And when you got back, Cocoa was gone?" Tristan concluded.

Shane nodded. "I th-thought Mum would be cr-cross if I said what really happened."

"Oh, Shane," Mrs Jupp said. "Don't be silly! You can always tell me the truth." She picked him up and the little boy wrapped his arms around her neck and clung to her, sobbing.

"What about the gate?" Andi asked. "Was it open, like you said?"

He shook his head.

The Pet Finders looked at each other. This changed things. Perhaps they needed to look a bit closer to home. They had focused their search farther away because there didn't seem to be any way Cocoa could have got out of the hutch or the garden on her own.

"Could we leave our dogs in your house while we

look around a bit more, Mrs Jupp?" asked Andi.

"You can put them in the kitchen," Mrs Jupp offered. "They'll be fine in there."

The Jupps' garden was basically a strip of grass surrounded by a concrete path edged with bushes. A shed stood near the end of the garden.

"Let's try the shed first," Andi said. 'Guinea pigs tend to get hot, so Cocoa might have gone in there for some shade." She opened the door. The shed was very tidy, with garden tools hung neatly on hooks. The floor was clear and they could see at once that Cocoa wasn't there.

"Let's search the bushes," Natalie suggested. She ran to the end of the garden nearest the house, Tristan headed for the gate, and Andi started searching in the middle. They crawled along on their hands and knees, lifting branches to peer underneath and calling Cocoa's name. But there was no sign of her.

"Hey!" Tristan called suddenly. 'There's a guinea pig-sized hole leading next door."

Andi ran to see. Tristan stood up, his eyes full of excitement. "And there's brown hair caught on the fence. She must have gone through!" He held out his hand to show a few strands of wiry, dark-brown hair.

Shane raced up. "That's her hair!"

Andi stood on tiptoe to look over the fence, then groaned. The grass on the other side was knee-high, and the borders were packed with tall flowers and weeds, with shrubs so bushy that a whole family of guinea pigs could be hiding inside them. "This is going to take a while," she sighed. But at least there was a chance that Cocoa might have been able to hide from cats and foxes in the miniature jungle.

"We'll have to go and ask your neighbour for permission to search his garden," Natalie said to Mrs Jupp.

"No need," Mrs Jupp told her. "He moved away a couple of months ago and the new people haven't moved in yet. Their back gate is unlocked. Shane has had to go in there a few times to find his football."

"Here goes then," Natalie sighed as they went next door. "I hope I don't stain my jeans."

They started by searching a flowerbed close to the hole in the fence. The flowers were tangled with thistles and weeds. "This would be a good place for her to hide," Tristan said. 'Guinea pigs are pretty nervous, so this tangle would make her feel safe."

"How come you're suddenly an expert on guinea pigs?" Natalie asked.

"I read up on them at Paws for Thought this

morning, while I was waiting for a delivery to arrive."

Andi spotted a dandelion with frilly leaves, looking as if it had been nibbled to death by sharp little teeth. She yanked it out of the ground. "Do guinea pigs eat dandelion leaves, Tris?"

"Love 'em," Tristan replied.

"She could have come this way then. Let's see if we can find any more."

There was another half-eaten dandelion growing under a rose bush, and a row of overgrown lettuce-like plants had tiny teeth marks all over them.

"Guinea pigs spend about six hours a day eating," Tristan told them. "Lucky for us, it means she's left us a trail to follow."

They kept searching. Natalie soon found that the base of a bird table had been gnawed. "She definitely came this way," she said. "Her tooth marks are really clear in this wood. Where was she heading?"

At last, Andi spotted a patch of wet mud where Cocoa's tiny paw prints were clearly visible. "She was definitely here for a while," she said. "Her claws have made pretty deep holes in the soil."

"I wonder if she's gone into that shed," Natalie said. "If she likes safe places, she might have sneaked in there. I'll see if the door's open."

At the same time, Andi bent back a bramble and crawled through a narrow gap between a rose bush and a clump of thorny shrubs, peering round in all directions for more evidence that the guinea pig had been that way.

Suddenly, she heard Natalie's voice again. "Come and see this!"

Andi stood up. Natalie was standing in the shed doorway. She was covered from head to toe in cobwebs and there was a dirty smudge on her nose, but she was wearing a huge grin.

Andi and Tristan raced over to her. "Have you found Cocoa?"

Natalie stood aside so that they could see past her into the shed. For a moment, after the sunny brightness of the garden, Andi couldn't make out anything. Then her eyes became accustomed to the gloom and she saw that the shed was almost empty. A workbench stood under a grimy window, covered with dust and webs. Beneath it was a pile of hessian sacks, and in the middle of the heap crouched Cocoa.

But not just Cocoa! Beside her were four tiny baby guinea pigs: two brown, one white, and one black.

"Oh!" Andi breathed. She crouched down beside the guinea pig nest and stroked Cocoa with one

finger. "It's okay, girl. We're going to take you and your babies home!"

"I didn't realize guinea pigs were born with their fur," Natalie whispered. "I thought they'd be hairless, like rats and mice." She bent down to pet the babies and they squirmed towards her, giving tiny squeaks.

"Do you think Cocoa will bite me if I pick her up?" Andi asked. She touched the guinea pig cautiously, but Cocoa didn't seem bothered, so she lifted her up. The guinea pig settled down in her hands so trustingly that Andi realized Shane must be a good guinea pig owner – even if he was a bit forgetful!

Natalie and Tristan each picked up two of the babies. Then they went out of the shed into the sunshine.

"I'm very impressed, Nat," Tristan said. "I would never have thought you'd go inside that filthy shed."

Natalie shrugged. "Someone had to do it. And I'm glad I did, as we've solved another case. Let's hope the dry cleaners do a good job with my clothes."

Tristan and Andi laughed, and Cocoa squeaked in alarm.

"Sorry, little one," Andi apologized.

As they went back into the Jupps' garden, Shane and his mum came running over quickly. "Did you find her?" Shane cried. "I thought I heard her squeaking!"

"She's here." Andi placed the guinea pig in his hands. Cocoa snuggled against him, giving tiny whooping murmurs, a bit like purring.

"She wasn't the only guinea pig we found," Natalie said. She and Tristan bent down so Shane could see the four babies.

"Babies!" he gasped. He turned to look at his mum, his eyes shining. "Mum, Cocoa's had babies!"

Mrs Jupp smiled weakly. 'What a surprise! I never would have guessed Cocoa was expecting. And we always thought Sugar was a girl." She sighed. "I suppose that means we'll need another hutch to keep the two of them apart."

"I sometimes help out at Paws for Thought, the pet shop in the high street," Tristan said. "I'm sure Christine Wilson, the owner, would be happy to swap Sugar for a girl guinea pig. And she'll take the babies, too, when they're old enough to leave their mother."

Mrs Jupp smiled. 'That sounds encouraging. But I'll have to talk to Shane about swapping Sugar. I'll put her – I mean *him* – in the glass tank indoors for now, where the guinea pigs live during the winter, so Cocoa and her babies don't have to share." She lifted Sugar out of the hutch gently. "Come on, girl – oops, boy," she corrected hastily. "You're coming inside with me." She headed towards the house, then stopped by the French doors and turned back to the Pet Finders. 'Thank you so much for all your help. You've done a great job."

"We enjoyed it," Andi said. "And I'm glad everything's turned out okay."

She opened the sleeping compartment of the hutch and Shane placed Cocoa inside. She turned in a little circle, flattening a nest in the hay. Tristan and Natalie put the babies in it, and Cocoa began to rearrange the hay around them to keep them warm.

"We'd better go," Natalie said, as Andi shut the hutch door again. She gazed down at her filthy clothes. "I really need a bath."

"Thanks for finding Cocoa!" Shane said, his eyes shining. "And the babies are lovely! I promise I'll never, ever leave them outside."

"Glad we could help," Tristan said.

They got the dogs from inside, then set off for the RSPCA to take the puppy back.

"This feels brilliant!" Tristan exclaimed. "We thought Cocoa was gone for good and, in the end, we found Shane four extra guinea pigs!"

"It's perfect!" Natalie agreed. "We've done it again!"

"But this time was different," Andi pointed out. 'We'll have to watch out for owners not telling the truth in the future. Where's that list of names, Tris?" she added. "Maybe our good luck with Cocoa will spill over into the puppy's case."

He fished it out and they all gathered around to look at it.

"Hang about, I recognize this name," Andi said. "Griffith. My friend Chen's always going on about his friend, Ashleigh Griffith. She lives next door to him. I wonder if it's her family who's moved, or some other Griffiths."

"Do you know where Chen lives?" Natalie asked.

"Oriel Way. I took a get-well card to him last week because he's had an ear infection."

"Would he know whether his neighbours had a dog or not?" Tristan asked.

"Of course," said Andi. "They were best friends."

"Shall we go there now?"

Andi nodded. "What are we waiting for?"

Chapter Eleven

"I can't go anywhere like this," Natalie wailed. "My reputation will be ruined if I turn up at Chen's house covered in cobwebs."

"We'll clean you up," Andi said. She picked a sticky cobweb off Natalie's shoulder. "You haven't got time to go home and change."

It didn't take long to brush the worst of the dust off Natalie's clothes. Andi wiped away the smudge from her nose and they set off on the short walk to Chen's house.

"I'll wait outside with the dogs," Natalie offered. "Perhaps our dog with no name will recognize her old home and give us a clue." She was obviously convinced she still wasn't presentable.

Chen's mother, Mrs Lu, showed them up to his bedroom. She seemed pleased that he had some visitors.

Chen was lying on his bed in pyjamas, watching television. Model aeroplanes hung from the ceiling and there were dozens of others half-built on his desk and chest of drawers.

His face brightened when they went in. "I'm really pleased to see you!" he said, switching off the television and sitting up. "I'm bored to death in here, but my mum thinks I'll get ill again if I don't rest."

"You could finish making one of these planes," Tristan suggested, picking up a wing.

Chen shrugged. "I've had enough of planes for a while. Sticking bits of plastic together is pretty much all I've been doing for the last week."

"Are you feeling better?" Andi asked.

"Tons. With any luck I'll be back at school on Monday."

Tristan gaped at him. "Are you kidding? You're actually looking forward to going back to school?"

"Yes! It's no fun being home now anyway. My friend Ashleigh from next door has moved away."

Andi and Tristan looked at each other excitedly. "I don't suppose she had a dog, did she?" Andi asked.

"Yeah. Her uncle bought her a puppy for her birthday. How did you know?"

"We've found a lost puppy and we think it might belong to someone who's moved away," Tristan explained.

"What breed was Ashleigh's puppy?" Andi asked.

"I don't know. I only caught a glimpse of it a couple of times. They only had it for a few weeks. Before we knew I had an ear infection, my mum thought it was my allergies that were causing my headaches, so I wasn't allowed to go and see the dog. I know it was yellow, though."

A mixture of hope and anxiety stirred inside Andi, and from the expression on Tristan's face, she could tell that he was feeling the same.

"When did Ashleigh move, Chen?" Tristan said.

"At the end of last week. Thursday, I think."

"We've got to get inside the house next door," Andi whispered.

"Good thinking," Tristan agreed. "We've got to go, Chen," he added abruptly.

Chen's face fell. "But you've only just got here."

"Sorry," Andi said. "This can't wait. We'll come back and see you later."

She and Tristan raced out of the room, downstairs, and out of the front door.

Natalie was sitting in the garden. Buddy and Jet

were lying beside her and the puppy was curled up in her arms, fast asleep.

"I tried to see if the puppy recognized the house, but I couldn't tell," she explained. "She looked excited for a minute, but then she just lay down and went to sleep. I wonder if it's because she's sad."

Andi and Tristan quickly explained what they'd learnt from Chen.

"Wow! Good work!" she exclaimed "We're getting really good at this, you know."

"Not so fast. We still need to find out what type of puppy Ashleigh had," Andi said. "Lots of breeds have yellowy fur. Come on!" She sprinted round to Chen's neighbour's house.

"What are we going to say?" Tristan asked, as Natalie rang the bell. "The new people might not know anything about Ashleigh's puppy."

"We've got to prove that she used to live here," Natalie said. "Then we can track the Griffiths down."

There was no time to say anything else, because the door was opened by a red-haired woman in her early thirties. "Hello," she said, smiling at them.

"I – um – that is, we . . ." Tristan looked around helplessly at the other Pet Finders.

Andi tried to think of something to say, but her

mind was blank. What sort of evidence might prove that the puppy had once lived here?

"Can we look for pet hair in your house, please?" Natalie said.

The woman's mouth dropped open. "Pet hair?" she echoed. "What on earth are you talking about?"

"We think a Labrador puppy used to live here," Andi added, afraid that the woman might close the door. "We're the Pet Finders Club and we're trying to find her owners. She's lost."

"I see. Well, you might be at the right address. My husband and I didn't see a dog when we looked at the house, but one must have moved in here after we'd agreed to buy. I'm allergic to dog hair and I sneezed non-stop for the first two days after we moved in."

"Can we come in then, please?" Andi asked. She crossed her fingers for luck. It would be terrible if the woman turned them away when they were so close to finding out the truth.

"I suppose you can, though I'm not sure you'll find anything. My husband went through the house with the vacuum cleaner. And you'll have to leave those dogs outside, I'm afraid."

"I'll hold them," Tristan offered. He took Jet's and

Buddy's leads, and Natalie carefully transferred the sleeping pup into his arms. She opened one eye and yawned widely, then settled down again with a contented sigh.

"I'm Mrs O'Donnell," the woman added.

"I'm Andi and this is Natalie," Andi said, as they stepped inside. She glanced around eagerly but, to her dismay, the house was spotless. "This place is even cleaner than your house, Nat," she whispered.

They followed Mrs O'Donnell from room to room. The living room and kitchen had polished wooden floors, and Andi and Natalie exchanged an anxious glance. "I don't think we'll find much fur here," Nat said in a low voice. "Hardwood floors are really easy to clean."

Upstairs, the bedrooms were carpeted and Andi's hopes soared. Surely there'd be a few hairs remaining here. She got down on her hands and knees in a corner of the second biggest bedroom, guessing that this might have been Ashleigh's room, but there wasn't a trace of hair to be found. They searched the other bedrooms, too, their anxiety growing by the second as they crawled backward and forward across the beige carpets.

"I didn't know my husband was so good at

vacuuming," Mrs O'Donnell laughed. 'I'll have to start renting him out."

"That's that then," Natalie said miserably, when they were standing in the hall again. "We've run out of leads."

"Hang on," Andi gasped. "What about the vacuum cleaner? I bet that will turn up some evidence!" She turned to Mrs O'Donnell. "Do you think we could look at your vacuum cleaner?"

"Well, if you really want to." She fetched it from the cupboard under the stairs. "But please take it outside if you're planning to empty it. The dustbin is round the side of the house."

Andi and Natalie hurried outside with the vacuum cleaner. "Any luck?" Tristan called.

"Not yet. But there might be some hair in here." Natalie disconnected the vacuum cleaner bag, then tipped the dirt on to a sheet of newspaper beside the dustbin.

"Bingo!" Andi whooped. Mixed in with the dust and fluff were hundreds of strands of yellow dog hair. Grinning broadly, she pulled out a small bunch of hairs and ran over to hold it against the puppy's coat. It was the wrong colour.

"Oh no!" Andi groaned. "She didn't belong to Ashleigh!"

"No, wait," Tristan said. "Her fur's paler underneath. Look." He tilted the puppy slightly and they saw that she was much lighter on her tummy. The pale hairs were a perfect match.

Natalie delved into the vacuum cleaner again. "These look darker," she said, pulling out a few strands of hair the colour of dark honey. She held them against the fur on the puppy's back. "The colour's identical here, as well. She must have lived in this house! Now we've got to find out whether she's lost or abandoned."

"We'll have to call her old owners," Tristan said. "Let's ask Chen if he's got Ashleigh's phone number."

"I'll go." Andi darted back to Chen's house and rang the bell.

By the time she came back, Tristan and Natalie had put the vacuum cleaner back together and returned it to Mrs O'Donnell.

"You could ring her on your mobile phone right now, Nat," Tristan said.

Natalie shook her head. "I don't think this is the sort of call we should make. Perhaps we should ask Fisher to do it. I mean, this is pretty serious stuff – especially if they deliberately dumped the puppy on that main road."

Tristan started to argue, but Andi interrupted. "Natalie's right. It would be best if Fisher phoned Ashleigh's mum."

"Let's go and ask him to do it now," Natalie said. Her voice shook and Andi squeezed her arm. She knew exactly how Natalie felt. They'd almost found the puppy's owner, but this was very different from solving their other cases. Finding *this* owner might not be a cause for celebration . . .

"Wow! This puppy weighs tons more than Lucy," Tristan complained as the Pet Finders reached the RSPCA. 'I'll be glad to put her down."

Fisher was in his office when they went inside. "Hello," he said. 'Good walk?"

"We think we've found out who owns the puppy!" Andi burst out. "It's a girl named Ashleigh Griffith."

"She moved to Pemberton," Tristan added. Pemberton was a town about an hour's drive from Aldcliffe.

Fisher put down his pen. "Have you spoken to her?"

"Not yet. It felt sort of – wrong for us to call."

Fisher understood what Andi meant. "You mean, in case her family deserted the puppy?"

They nodded, almost ashamed to agree.

"OK," said Fisher. "Give me the phone number and I'll speak to Ashleigh's mum or dad."

Andi read it out to him and he jotted it down on a message pad. "Right. You three go and put the puppy back in her cage and I'll come to find you when I've finished."

The puppy had a drink of water, then flopped contentedly into her basket and fell asleep. Buddy lay down beside the open cage door while Jet licked her empty food bowl and looked hopefully up at Natalie.

"What do you think Fisher's saying?" Andi wondered, glancing at the door. "I really hope the puppy was only lost and that Ashleigh wants her back. She wouldn't have seen the posters or the newspaper in Pemberton." But there was a nagging doubt at the back of her mind: if Ashleigh loved the puppy so much, why hadn't she reported her missing?

"This case is the most difficult we've ever had," Tristan sighed. "Trying to find an owner who might not want to be found—" He broke off as Fisher appeared in the doorway. "What did they say?"

He sighed. "It's no-go. I'm really sorry. I spoke to Mrs Griffith earlier. She says they haven't got a dog – never have."

"But that's not true!" Natalie exclaimed. "We saw the puppy's fur in Mrs O'Donnell's vacuum cleaner."

"I know, it looks suspicious," Fisher agreed, "but all golden Labs have hair about this colour. Perhaps another golden Lab visited the Griffiths before they moved." He shrugged. "It was a great lead, but to be honest, I don't see what else I can do. I've got to take Mrs Griffith's word that they've never had a dog." The phone started to ring then, and he went to answer it.

"That means we still don't know for sure who the puppy's owner is," Andi said miserably. "This is hopeless! We can't find a new home for her until we know that her old owner definitely doesn't want her back."

"I suppose we just got it wrong and we'll have to keep searching," Tristan said.

"But we know Ashleigh had a puppy because Chen said so," Andi pointed out. "Mrs Griffith *must* be lying!"

"That's right!" Natalie said fiercely. "We'll just have to make the Griffiths admit that the puppy belonged to them!"

Andi frowned. 'But how?"

There had to be a way. If only they could work out what it was . . .

Chapter Twelve

"Lunch," Tristan said. "That's what we need."

"How can you think about food at a time like this?" Natalie challenged him. "We've just reached a dead end in our search for the puppy's owner and all you're worried about is eating."

"We need to think," Tristan pointed out. "And it's already two o'clock. I always think better on a full stomach."

"We might as well go," Andi said. "Hanging around here's not going to change anything."

They said a quick goodbye to the puppy and headed outside. "There's a baker's on the corner," Tristan said. "Let's get some sandwiches and eat them in the park. Then we can talk about what to do next."

They found an empty bench near the pond. Andi didn't feel much like eating, so she shared her cheese and tomato roll with Buddy. She was angry and frustrated. What they needed was to speak to Ashleigh: perhaps then they'd find out the truth about the puppy. But if she phoned Ashleigh, she might tell the same story as her mum. Who knew what was going on?

Suddenly she had a brainwave. "I know!"

Tristan and Natalie turned to her eagerly. 'What?"

"I'll ring Ashleigh and offer her the dog-training DVD I used when Buddy was a puppy. I'll tell her I know Chen so she won't be suspicious."

"Here, use my mobile." Natalie handed it to her and Andi punched in the number. She held her breath, willing Ashleigh to pick it up.

"Hello?" said a girl's voice after a few rings.

"Can I speak to Ashleigh, please?" Andi asked.

"This is Ashleigh."

"Oh hello, my name's Andi. I'm a friend of Chen's. He told me you've got a new puppy and I wondered if you'd like my dog-training DVD. It worked wonders with my Jack Russell, Buddy." She glanced round for Buddy and saw him chasing ducks at the edge of the pond. The ducks were waddling away as fast as they could. "Of course, I know your dog isn't a terrier . . ." Andi paused, hoping Ashleigh would say something.

"No, she was a golden Labrador. But I haven't got her any more. My uncle bought her for me without checking that we actually wanted a dog first. I tried really hard to look after her, but it was impossible to fit everything in. I play the flute and I go to gymnastics, too. And then there's homework. Luckily my mum managed to find a new home for the puppy."

"Oh." Andi gave Tristan and Natalie a cautious thumbs-up. "When? Chen didn't tell me that."

"We moved last week and I went to stay with my grandparents for a few days while my mum and dad organized everything. When I came back, the puppy was gone."

"You must have been really upset when you found out," Andi said, imagining how she'd feel if her mum gave Buddy away.

"I was sad at first," Ashleigh agreed. "But I know it's for the best. Puppies need a lot of attention and I just couldn't give her as much time as I wanted."

"You won't need the DVD, then."

"No. Thanks for asking, though. Bye."

Andi hung up, pressing the off button much harder than she needed to. She wasn't angry with Ashleigh, but the way Mrs Griffith had acted made Andi's blood boil.

"What did she say?" Tristan asked.

"Is the puppy hers?" Natalie demanded.

"Yes, but Ashleigh didn't have enough time to look after her properly," Andi blurted out. "Mrs Griffith told Ashleigh that she'd found a new home for the puppy – so it must have been her who dumped her!"

"You didn't tell her that the puppy's turned up?" Natalie said.

"No!" There was no way she was going to tell Ashleigh that the puppy had been found, in case the Griffiths decided they wanted her back after all. The puppy deserved a home where people had time for her!

Buddy trotted over, and Andi picked him up and hugged him. He licked her chin.

"Let's go back to the clinic and tell Fisher what we've found out," Tristan said. "Did Ashleigh tell you the puppy's name, Andi?"

Andi stared at him in dismay. 'I forgot to ask!"

The Pet Finders took Buddy and Jet home before heading back to the RSPCA. Andi needed a walk to calm herself down: talking to Ashleigh had upset her more than she wanted to admit.

Fisher was on the phone when they arrived. They waited outside his office door until he hung up. "This phone hasn't stopped ringing since you left," he said. 'Just about all of Aldcliffe saw the puppy in the paper and wants to offer her a home." He laughed. "It looks like you'll have to hold interviews if you don't manage to find her real owner first."

"Oh, we've found her real owner, all right," Tristan said grimly.

The Pet Finders told Fisher about Andi's phone call to Ashleigh. He sighed and shook his head. "If only people would make sure pets are wanted before they give them as presents! Still, we can treat the puppy as a stray now and find her a new home." His attention was diverted to the window then. "Who's this?"

Through the window, they saw that a red car had pulled up outside. A tall woman in a blue dress climbed out. She hurried towards the door of the building.

"I'm Mrs Griffith," she said anxiously, as she breezed into the reception area and approached the desk. "I've come to see Mr Pearce."

"It's Ashleigh's mum!" Natalie hissed.

Andi's knees felt as if they were going to buckle. There could only be one reason why Mrs Griffith had turned up at the RSPCA – she'd guessed that the puppy had been found and now she'd changed her mind and wanted her back.

"Quick!" Andi said. "In here!"

The Pet Finders darted into the animal unit. The puppy was still asleep. "We've got to get her out of here," Andi decided. "There's no way she's going home with *that* woman."

They opened the cage door. "Come on, girl!" Natalie picked her up.

"Hang on," Tristan warned. "We're Pet *Finders*, not pet*nappers*."

"Do you want her to go back to someone who dumped her on a main road?" Andi demanded.

Tristan shook his head, took the puppy from Natalie and tucked her inside his jacket. She popped her head out and licked his chin.

Natalie pushed her down again. "You've got to stay in there," she warned her. "It won't be for long, I promise."

"Come on," Andi said. They hurried to the door and Andi opened it. To her dismay, Mrs Griffith was talking to Fisher in the corridor that led to the reception area. They'd have to walk right past her.

"I wasn't entirely truthful with you on the phone

earlier, Mr Pearce," Mrs Griffith said. "We did have a puppy, but I lost her. And when you phoned I couldn't say anything because my daughter was there. You see, I told her I'd found a new home for her puppy but—" She spotted the Pet Finders and stopped.

"Hello," Andi said, forcing herself to smile. She knew there was no way Mrs Griffith would know her, but she couldn't help feeling scared. She walked along the corridor, trying to look casual, and squeezed past Mrs Griffith. Tristan started to follow but the puppy gave a tiny yap from inside his jacket.

The Pet Finders froze. Fisher's eyebrows shot so high they almost vanished into his hair.

"We're – um . . ." Tristan began, trailing off as the puppy's head appeared just below his chin.

"Taking her out for some exercise," Natalie finished for him.

"She looked as though she needed some fresh air," Andi added hurriedly.

Mrs Griffith gasped when she spotted the puppy. "Oh! You've found her! I'm so relieved." She ruffled the puppy's silky ears. "I've been so worried about her."

"Come into my office," Fisher said.

Mrs Griffith went inside with him and sat down on a chair by his desk. The Pet Finders followed and perched on the windowsill. The puppy gazed around with her soft little ears pricked up.

"What actually happened?" Fisher asked.

"I was bringing the puppy here, last Thursday, the day we moved to Pemberton. I know you can find homes for unwanted pets. I stopped for petrol but I couldn't have closed my car door properly. The puppy escaped. I realized she was missing as soon as I went back to my car."

Andi's anger towards Mrs Griffith began to subside a little. Perhaps she wasn't quite as bad as she'd feared.

"I searched for ages," Mrs Griffith continued, "up and down all the roads around the petrol station, but there was no sign of her. And I kept thinking of all the things I still had to do – last-minute packing, organizing the removal men, getting the house ready for the new people who were moving in," she sighed, "and picking my daughter up from her grandparents'. In the end, I had to give up the search and go home."

"I see," Fisher said. "Why didn't you report her missing?"

Mrs Griffith swallowed hard. "I thought about it, but everything has been such a rush. I've hardly had a moment to myself. And Ashleigh, my daughter, has been home, helping me get organized. She starts her new school on Monday. I told her I'd found a home for the puppy, so she wouldn't be upset. I didn't want her to overhear me phoning the RSPCA and telling them that the puppy was lost."

"So you don't want the puppy back?" Andi checked. Although she knew now that the Griffiths weren't as bad as she'd feared, she was certain they weren't the right owners for the little Lab.

"Oh, no," Mrs Griffith said hurriedly. "We never wanted a dog in the first place. My brother just turned up with her on Ashleigh's birthday. And then my husband got a job as a restaurant manager in Pemberton, and things started to get hectic. We promised the people buying our house that we'd be out by the first, and before I knew it, it was the thirtieth! We had to leave quickly, and we're living in a flat above the restaurant – only temporarily, but there's no way we can have a dog there."

"So you'll be happy to let us re-home her for you?" Fisher asked.

"Oh, yes, please. It would be such a weight off my mind."

Fisher took a form out of his desk drawer and set it in front of Mrs Griffith. "You'll need to fill this out."

"Of course. And can I give you a cheque to cover

the cost of any treatment you've given the puppy?"

"A donation to the centre would be welcome," Fisher said smiling.

Mrs Griffith filled in the form, then wrote out a cheque and handed it to him.

"Thank you." Fisher tucked the cheque into the pocket of his white coat. "And don't worry about the puppy. She appeared in the local paper this week and we've been inundated with calls from people who want to give her a home."

"I'm so pleased," Mrs Griffith said. She stood up and stroked the puppy's head. "She's a dear little thing, and I'm really glad I came now. I had to come back to Aldcliffe to get the last of our things. I'd left them in a friend's garage." She headed for the door.

As she went out, Mike Morgan came in. "How's the world's sweetest puppy today?" he asked, smiling round at them.

"She's great," Andi told him. "And we've tracked down her owner!"

Mike's smile froze on his lips. "Oh." He sounded disappointed. "I've kind of got used to visiting her. I'm going to miss her when she's gone."

"Don't worry, the previous owner doesn't want her back," Natalie told him.

"So, I'll be able to see her for a bit longer?"

"Yes," Fisher agreed.

"Do you know what?" Tristan groaned. "We didn't ask Mrs Griffith the puppy's name."

"Well, whatever she's called, I've brought her some corncobs," Mike said. He spotted the pup peeping out of Tristan's jacket. "Hello, girl." He reached in to stroke her. "How are you?"

The dog with no name scrabbled her way out of Tristan's jacket and launched herself at him. Mike caught her, laughing, and held her close to his chest. "I guess you'll be looking for a new home for her now," he said.

Suddenly, Andi knew the perfect person to adopt the puppy. "You should have her, Mike!" she said. "You two are perfect together!"

"Me!" Mike's face lit up. Then his smile faded. "But I've never had a pet. I don't know the first thing about looking after a dog."

"You can learn. There are hundreds of books about caring for dogs," Fisher said, and handed him a leaflet. "And there are the dog-training classes I run with Christine Wilson."

"And Christine can give you information about feeding and everything," Tristan added.

"And you can do your marathon-training together!" Andi pointed out. "That puppy needs lots of exercise! It'll keep her out of mischief."

"And during the day, when I'm out on my rounds, she can keep everyone company at the depot." Mike was clearly warming to the idea. "Tony, one of the sorters, loves dogs. He'd be thrilled to keep an eye on her."

"It's perfect!" Natalie declared. "How about it, Fisher? Can Mike have her?"

The puppy stretched up and licked Mike's ear.

Fisher smiled. "It looks like she's chosen her new owner for herself," he said. "And I'd hate to disappoint her."

Mike's smile stretched even wider. "Wow!" he beamed, hugging the puppy tightly. "Do you hear that, girl? You're coming home with me!"

"Hang on a minute!" said Andi, holding up her hand. "You're forgetting one very important thing!"

Mike looked up and frowned. "What? I can get her a basket and a lead on the way home, can't I?"

"Nothing like that," Andi said with a grin. "This little pup may have found her new home, but we never found her a new name!'

153

THE PET FINDERS CLUB

Searching for Sunshine

Do you love animals?
Has your pet ever gone missing?

Well meet Andi, Tristan and Natalie —
The Pet Finders Club. Animals don't stay
lost for long with them hot on the trail!

Andi and Natalie love having horse-riding
lessons, until their favourite pony is
stolen! Sunshine isn't even the most
valuable horse at the stables; it
doesn't make any sense. Are there
horse-thieves in the area? The Pet
Finders are determined to find out!